OLUWALE NOW

ACKNOWLEDGEMENTS

Cover artwork: 'Hibiscus Rising' by Jeannine Mellonby from A to B films. Based on the sculpture *Hibiscus Rising* by Yinka Shonibare, CBE, RA and created with kind permission from the Shonibare Studio, 2023.

Ian Duhig – 'An Aroko for David Oluwale' first published in *Ten Poems About Rivers* (Candlestick, 2018)

Nnadi Samuel – 'Schwa: In a sound where all Consonants means Loss' previously published online at bywords.ca, (2022)

OLUWALE NOW

An Anthology of Poetry, Prose and Artwork
responding to the Story of David Oluwale

Edited by

EMILY ZOBEL MARSHALL
SAI MURRAY

Foreword by

CARYL PHILLIPS

PEEPAL TREE

First published in Great Britain in 2023
Peepal Tree Press Ltd
17 King's Avenue
Leeds LS6 1QS
UK

ISBN 978 1 845235 81 9

Printed in the United Kingdom

Supported using public funding by
ARTS COUNCIL
ENGLAND

CONTENTS

LOST

WHO CARES NOW?

TOWARDS HOPE

INTRODUCTION

EMILY ZOBEL MARSHALL, SAI MURRAY

Remembering Oluwale

Let us situate David Oluwale in the city of Leeds. The killing of George Floyd by Minneapolis police officer Derek Chauvin on May 25th, 2020, which sparked the global Black Lives Matter protests, carries strong echoes of the tragedy of David's killing. David arrived in Hull in East Yorkshire in 1949 as a stowaway in a cargo ship from Lagos. Like all migrants, he travelled in hope of a brighter future. But from 1953 to 1969 he suffered from homelessness, racism, destitution, police persecution and mental ill-health. David, after a sustained and brutal pattern of abuse, was hounded to death by two police officers, drowned in the river Aire in 1969 near Leeds Bridge. Recent events have shown us that Leeds, like many other cities in the UK, has become less openly hostile towards migrants, but that racist and discriminatory attitudes persist.

British Caribbean author Caryl Phillips grew up in working-class areas of Leeds, revisits the story of David Oluwale in his historical fiction 'Northern Lights' in *Foreigners: Three English Lives* (2008). Whilst in conversation with Professor John McLeod in Leeds in 2015, Phillips explained:

> Leeds rejected Oluwale. Friends and social work agencies tried to help, but there is no getting around the fact that the city looked the other way while this man was cast – literally – onto the waters. But back in the late 1960s the city was busy, and the city stood on the threshold of a transformation that has finally come to pass.

[…] How would David Oluwale, or any newcomer, fare in today's regeneration Leeds? […]. The temperature of the water remains the same. The river remains the same. The water tells the story. Without the river there would be no Leeds. The same river down which David Oluwale made his fateful final journey to his resting place in a clump of weeds near the Knostrop Sewage Works. [2015; 883]

Phillips continually reminds us in his writing that the past inhabits the present. He states: 'I think we're all of us guilty of walking right past the evidence of our history and the specific evidence of our colonial history, every day' (2015: 888). Phillip's warning, in 2015, that today the 'temperature of the water remains the same in Leeds,' foreshadow the shocking events of April 2022. The David Oluwale Memorial Association, after a decade-long campaign, erected a blue plaque to commemorate Oluwale's life and death. Phillips travelled from the US to unveil the plaque and his words formed a part of the inscription (see image below):

The unveiling ceremony saw over two hundred people from across Leeds come together in solidarity and in support of social change. Hours after the plaque was unveiled by Phillips on Leeds Bridge, positioned at the point where David Oluwale is believed to have entered the water, it was stolen. This followed a racist incident on the bridge during the ceremony itself and a spate of graffiti on the foundations of the new Oluwale bridge, further upstream, and outside the Civic Trust offices, where the plaque was manufactured. The words read 'N*****s Out', and 'N*****s out of the UK'.

The night following the theft of the plaque, we had organised an in-conversation event entitled 'Oluwale Matters' with the David Oluwale Memorial Association [DOMA] and Leeds Beckett University at The Leeds Library with Caryl Phillips. Emily Zobel Marshall asked Caryl about his response to the events the night before and the theft of the plaque. He responded:

> We just saw something last night that Leeds doesn't want us to see, but that doesn't mean that Leeds is worse than any other city. There are always going to be uncomfortable narratives that exist within the framework of our city. It's not about what happened last night that is the issue, quite honestly, it's what we are going to do now, and we are going to do something. It's not what was done to us, it's what we are going to do in return.
>
> Talking to you, Emily, and talking to Max [Farrar], it's clear we are not going to just roll over and do nothing. We already know about the uncomfortable truth that this highlights. We will [now] regroup – and we will get on with it.
>
> (Caryl Philips and Emily Zobel Marshall, 26th April 2022)

Since the removal of the plaque, the city has indeed 'got on with it'. There has been an overwhelming show of support from communities across Leeds for the work of the DOMA charity and an even louder call to 'Remember Oluwale'. A temporary, laminated plaque was put in the place of the stolen plaque the following day by councillors, and when this too was ripped in half, another was placed in the same spot.

A billboard company contacted the Leeds Civic Trust to ask if they could project the image of the plaque across the city on their electronic billboards. Leeds Civic Trust organised a Crowdfunder which raised over £3,000 over the next few days. Leeds Market projected a large image of David Oluwale's face and the plaque in their recreation hall. The plaque appeared on the big screen at the centre of the Millennium Square, in the city centre. There was increased fundraising for the DOMA charity, support from MPs and an outpouring of support from the general public, particularly through social media channels. The message has been clear; you can remove the plaque, but you cannot silence the message.

David Oluwale was a migrant who entered into an environment so hostile that he was denied the right to exist. His presence was so abhorrent to Inspector Geoffrey Ellerker and Sergeant Kenneth Kitchen that they sought to destroy him piecemeal and succeeded in doing so. This message of hostility clearly still permeates our city and British society today, expressed clearly in the graffiti daubed on the walls in Leeds. Yet the message of welcome to newcomers, to those perceived, by some, as foreigners or outsiders, is gaining strength.

photo © JC Deceaux

On November 25th 2023 a landmark sculpture entitled *The David Oluwale Memorial: Hibiscus Rising* by world famous British-Nigerian artist Yinka Shonibare, commissioned by DOMA, was unveiled in Meadow Lane, Aire Park, Leeds. The cover art for this book is inspired by the hibiscus flower which echoes throughout Yinka's incredible work and ties the Oluwale narrative to his West African roots. This will be one of the first pieces of public art in the city which reflects its diverse cultures and ensures that we always remember Oluwale.

Yoruba Heritage Group Yorkshire performing at the Hibiscus Rising opening on 25th November 2023 with Chloe Hudson, DOMA secretary (in red)

The *Oluwale Now* Anthology

What is it about David Oluwale's story that has moved so many artists, singers, writers and poets to respond to his life? While the media and academia are only just starting to explore this question, it is the creatives, the thinkers and dreamers who have taken on the task of drawing attention to the horrors of the past, of ensuring that we never forget David Oluwale.

Oluwale Now is an anthology of poetry, prose and artwork exploring the contemporary issues that David Oluwale's story touches upon. Building upon *Remembering Oluwale: An Anthology* (edited by SJ Bradley, Valley Press, 2016 – the first collection of writing responding to the Oluwale story) this book centres the themes of memory, belonging, otherness and optimism. Abolitionist futures cannot be built without cessation of the consequences of past and ongoing abuses of power. The writing here combats historical silencing. It places the voices of the marginalised centre stage.

We received over 80 prose and poetry submissions responding to David's life and exploring issues that his story touches upon, such as the city of Leeds, marginalisation, racial justice, mental ill-health, rough-sleeping, exclusion, resistance and hope. The process of selecting the winners and the pieces for publication was conducted over several rounds with up to seven volunteers (including Nasser Hussain, Alison Taft, James McGrath, Max Farrar, Jeremy Poynting) reading the submissions and Caryl Phillips selecting the overall winner Hannah Stone; second prize-winner Gill Tennant and runner-up Gayathiri Kamalakanthan.

The anthology is ordered into four sections, each named after one of the pieces of poetry or prose featured. The first section, 'Holding Memory', explores themes of memory and water; the way that memory, like water, sustains us, and like rivers, we can follow or track them back to their source.. Bookmarked by a selection of the harrowing police photos that were used at David's manslaughter trial, the work here begins with the travels of migrants across continents, journeys into the past, unpacking our longing to belong, and reminding us that to the unhoused, nature can be cold and hostile.

'Lost' begins with four artistic and colourful renderings of the only known photograph of David. The writings delve into themes of loneliness, isolation of homelessness, racism and the ill mental health suffered by David still central to the problems our communities face today. The colour and empathy in these stories humanise and, as Gill Tennant's story does, remind us: those who are displaced to the margins can still find 'joy' and that in their rejection of/ from the mainstream there can even be 'a kind of freedom and a happiness'.

'Who Cares Now?' tackles police brutality and prejudice head on. Bold, stark and arresting graphic artwork addresses what Brian Phillip calls 'agents of the establishment'. This section urges us all to think about the most marginalised in our society: whose stories are silenced, who move through our cities unnoticed or persecuted. The stories and poems in this section burn with the injustice of ongoing police brutality and prejudice and call for acknowledgment and action.

'Towards Hope', our final section, begins with David reimagined as a joyful carnival king, together with 'migrant masqueraders' in hibiscus flower costumes for the 50th Leeds West Indian Carnival. The writings call on us to claim birthrights, to uproot fear, sow love, and to forge pathways home. They show us that there is a future we must all fight for. That we must keep the dream alive, together, of a more socially and racially just society.

Why *Oluwale Now*?
In the period that this book has been written we have seen abhorrent political policies mooted such as: housing asylum seekers on off-shore barges; the demonisation of migrants seeking better lives who arrive in small boats; shipping desperate people in need of sanctuary thousands of miles overseas to client state countries; calls to remove tents from homeless people; and the increasing policing of, and clamp down of, protest in solidarity with oppressed peoples. Over half a century since David's body was found in the river Aire, can we be certain that we would not allow another person to suffer David Oluwale's fate today?

Remembering Oluwale now, means not forgetting those who are on the margins today. It means working to ensure that the reception of those making journeys to our shores and cities today is grounded in an analysis and understanding of the unjust legacies of colonial power that still remain at large; and which still ravage the lands of those in the global south. It means reckoning with the need to transform the lives of people living with mental ill-health and/or sleeping rough, and ensuring that police officers are accountable to and in service to the community at all times.

As these stories and poems illustrate and as the artwork reminds – there is still abundant empathy, compassion and energy that we must take heart and spirit from. Coming together in Leeds, in activism, in art and in literature, in the sharing of songs and stories, our voices can connect across the page and across oceans. We can be reminded of our shared humanity; we can remember the happier times experienced by David, and we can use our protest and our joy as a form of resistance against those that wish to dehumanise us and the marginalised people we stand alongside.

FOREWORD

CARYL PHILLIPS

As an eleven-year-old schoolboy growing up in Leeds, each morning I would undertake a long bus journey from Whinmoor to the city centre, where my school was located. I first made this journey in September 1969. Five months earlier, in April 1969, a man named David Oluwale had been killed in the city centre. The story had been widely reported in newspapers and on television. It was clear, even to my eleven-year-old senses, that the city of Leeds was somewhat traumatized by the death of this David Oluwale.

During the next two years, this sense of trauma deepened as an external police investigation was opened into what exactly what had transpired that had caused this man to lose his life. The results of the investigation were shocking, and eventually two police officers stood trial and were subsequently jailed for their part in the death of David Oluwale. Their gross behaviour had gone way beyond any authority granted to them by their uniform or their badge.

David Oluwale arrived in Leeds in 1949, a teenage stowaway on a ship from Nigeria that had docked at Hull. In those days, it was customary for stowaways to receive a mandatory short sentence, which was often served at Armley Jail, here in Leeds. Upon his release, David found lodgings near the university and secured a job in a car factory in Hunslet. The young man hoped to one day become an engineer, but it wasn't to be.

On an almost daily basis, the Leeds City Police force targeted David Oluwale. Young hooligans mercilessly taunted him. But David always answered back. As a result, David Oluwale ended up being dispatched to the other place of incarceration that was meant to control those who didn't know their place – the mental asylum, in this case the one at Menston, where he remained for eight years. Once discharged, David had nowhere to live and so he took to the streets of Leeds, sleeping in shop doorways and wherever he could find shelter. Inevitably, the police brutality began again, and this time it escalated.

In April 1969, two Leeds City police officers chased a terrified David Oluwale, through the city centre streets, and somehow David, a man who couldn't swim, ended up in the river. There were no witnesses. David Oluwale drowned.

During the short, thirty-nine, years of his life many people and institutions in this city neglected David Oluwale. He was an immigrant; he was homeless; he was plagued with psychological problems; he was black. These are facts. To some he was invisible; the man in the street you quickly step around as you avert your eyes. To others, he was simply a dishevelled nuisance. An embarrassing blot on the landscape. However, over the years, the evidence of David's life, and the ugly reality of his death have proved instructive, forcing this city to confront many uncomfortable truths.

Because of David Oluwale, I think we have a better understanding of ourselves; our short sightedness; our forgetfulness; our inability to take responsibility for the ills in our city; our cowardice. As a city we failed him, but let's learn from this and not fail ourselves. We are – all of us – social animals; we live in communities; and we have a deep responsibility to look out for those among us who are weak and suffering. Animals do this; just what kind of animals are we if we fail to do this for our fellow human beings?

During the past decade or so, the David Oluwale Memorial Association has done astonishing work in this city to focus our collective minds on the legacy of the life and death of David Oluwale. They have paid particular, but not exclusive, attention to issues associated with migration, homelessness, racism, and mental health. Their work is ongoing but today, together with the Leeds Civic Trust, they offer us a wonderful, and permanent, tribute to the life of this citizen of Leeds, in the form of a Blue Plaque.

However, one final thought. We should remember that David Oluwale's life may have ended right here in Leeds, but like all immigrants to our city, his journey began elsewhere. Across the water, in Nigeria. In 1949, his parents and siblings said goodbye to a brave ambitious teenager who was ready to depart for England. We owe his parents a moment of quiet reflection. Your teenage son came to us, and thereafter endured a difficult twenty years in our city. We could have done more. We should have done more. But we do remember your David. In fact, we have learned from him. And today, here in Leeds, we honour your son.

Transcript of speech delivered in Aire Park, Leeds, for the inauguration of a Leeds Civic Trust Blue Plaque for David Oluwale, 25th April 2022.

HOLDING MEMORIES

Leeds, UK, 1971, Middleton Woods, 4 miles from centre of Leeds   David dumped here on 11.8.68
[Prosecution photo for the trial of Ellerker and Kitching for the manslaughter of David Oluwale]

2

Leeds, UK, 1971, city centre: Entrance to John Peters Store on Lands Lane, where David often slept.
[Prosecution photo for the trial of Ellerker and Kitching for the manslaughter of David Oluwale]

2

Leeds, UK, 1971, Fox & Hounds pub, Bramhope, 5.5 miles from centre of Leeds   David dumped there on 7.8.68
[Prosecution photo for the trial of Ellerker and Kitching for the manslaughter of David Oluwale]   around 3.15 am

1

Leeds, UK, 1971, Call Lane, showing Warehouse Hill, leading to River Aire where David was last seen around 5am on
Text
18.4.69   [Prosecution photo for the trial of Ellerker and Kitching for the manslaughter of David Oluwale]

2

Leeds, UK, 1971, The River Aire at Knostrop, where David's body was found on 4.5.69. View from the bridge. [Prosecution photo for the trial of Ellerker and Kitching for the manslaughter of David Oluwale]

4

Leeds, UK, 1971. River Aire, looking upstream towards Leeds Bridge.
[Prosecution photo for the trial of Ellerker and Kitching for the manslaughter of David Oluwale]

6

CHIWENITE ONYEKWELU

THERE ARE MEMORIES I CARRY

(for uncle Peter & for David Oluwale)

About water   about the brothers
    sunk & drowning. I go

back to where their memories began.
    In every depth, a steel ship.

The port opens   & a man I love
    walks into the ocean in

search of hope. My mother calls him
    Peter   calls him brother

calls him every name we imagine
    would bring him home. This is the

twenty-sixth year, she says, & then
    silence– the way grief

renders the mouth motionless.   At Hull
    – 1949 – a cargo ship returns

from Lagos, thick & slippery. In its
    stomach there is a young

Nigerian flattened, his shirt rumpled.
    Just like my uncle, you could

see the dreams in his pristine eyes.
    When home is a field, burning   there

is nothing left to do but to leave. I know,
    because I have prayed for

water   & I have prayed for ship. But
    my mother says, *even the shores*

are harder than you think. How, after
    he left, my uncle phoned

to say he was homesick. Never before has
    he been judged by the

colour of his skin.   Never before   this
    hunger & this homelessness.

I do not know the noun for it, but
    here was a mind unravelling   a man

severed from himself. In Igbo we say
    mmiri & mean *water*. We

say it & what we mean is *life*. This is
    what I want eagerly to do –

to look beyond their wounds & see the
    men for the lives they lived.

See their eyes radiant with hope   the
    sweats they drew   the racism

police cuffs   the freedom they bought
    for other Blacks with their

own blood. Memory itself is enough
    weight, so I want the

joy part, the part where triumph enunciates.
    Where the names –

fresh as ever – are still carved deeply
    along the shores.

ROSARY

Our Father, Oluwale's pockets were full,
2 watery photos (spectres of home)
2 after-care forms (no care provided)
11 shillings and 10 pence (for tea and a bun)
your silver crucifix on turquoise rosary beads
fingered smooth by hope.
Glory be?

Our Father, Oluwale's heart was emptied
found by boys fishing near the sewage works
dreaming of dappled trout.
An unnamed body
floating on the Aire,
his love beaten out.
A policeman's triumph,
a deep-sunk story.
Glory be?

Our Father, Oluwale's bridge was bursting
with the people gathered
left with only traces,
fragments of a man,
but assembling the pieces
filling in the spaces
leaflets in their pockets
to Remember Oluwale.
Glory be.

IAN DUHIG

AN AROKO FOR DAVID OLUWALE

Oluwale is Yoruba for '*God Has Come Home*'
but he came to find Hell in God's Own Country,
no home but cold Leeds streets or police cells,
in his asylum only electroconvulsive therapy.

Now by the Aire, where David drowned fleeing
policemen's boots, his feet light from hunger,
my small nomadic cowrie garden grows for one
who'd grown to be a shell of himself in this city.

An empty cowrie is full as an egg with meanings:
Gods' eyes, they make *arokos*, magic messages.
Because *efa*, Yoruba for six, has the same letters
as the word to draw, my six cowries set down here

draw David's Christian ghost into Oshun's arms,
water Goddess with a name of water, that he too
might step into the true meaning of his own name
borne back to Africa where the river of us all rose.

This alchemy of cold fire on the Aire's earth makes
nothing happen, like poetry, yet makes something
from nothing for a man treated like he was nothing,
making room to reflect on river water running softly.

DEAR DAVID

Bodies of water are a rib
exposed veil between here and there.
Sometimes people are bodies of water.
Rarer, still,
water is time, is bodies, is people.

It is 03:00 a.m.
and water drips into my dreams still.
Sleep is a body under water, over and above,
a ship is chained to the sky.
Thirteen thousand kilometres of ocean is still
not a river.

I am in Leeds, praying to the River Aire.
It is not my water but somewhere down there
drowned David Oluwale.
A ship is chained to the bottom of a body
and a cop sweats tonight – dreams of a rib exposed,
flooding.

And maybe the body is enough,
is time and water.
And all the bodies that don't belong to me
climb into the poem
and find themselves home.

CHRIS SOWE

GANNEX MOUND

From snow-tinged blackness across the way, the Gannex mound materialised.
Scrunched balls of Evening Post hold precious warmth, beneath the coat my father wore.

"He's here Dad!" I'd call.

Gannex Mound, rustles and sways, it brushes me as he passes.

Down he'd go, carrying my fear.
Down past the blue book of Africa, it's musty pages,
scarifications and naked breasts always present at the turn.

In the cellar, bathed in gloomy incandescence, straw bails and tea chests build the scene.
Poised on boxes, plates and wares, two men share food and time.
No hark, no herald angels.
Never a room at the inn for Oluwale.

I hear my fathers words from 1969 . . .
"The Police. It was the Police! They've hounded him for years"

Suspected of being Black.
Guilty as charged.
Sentenced by two.
Appeal denied.
Take him down.
Deep into the white-tinged Blackness.

TALLAWAH

(for Lee Arbouin: a fierce champion for justice, 1943-2022)

She uses water to baptise her throat,
before evoking some of the memories she has indexed.
She thinks back to the swaggering man,
who draped up a boy and slapped him about the face,
when buttons flew from his shirt she shouted,
Hey! Hey! Hey!

Someone has to stoke the fire.

Anger made her draw for her eyebrow pencil,
mark the number plate on her arm,
and charge to the police station, kid in tow.
This thug would get what's coming and all the rest of it.
The boy's father didn't want to press charges,
afraid they'd plant ganja on him. Her husband warned
she had enough on her plate. The police kept asking:
What's it got to do with you?

Someone has to stoke the fire.

The lawyer pushed for the police
to uphold the law, but they wouldn't crack.
The mother didn't want any more crap on her doorstep.
So, the kid went home – unlike David Oluwale – knowing
some inclines are far too steep. Although age now
bulges around her middle, her war cry remains in tune.

Someone has to stoke the fire.

LYDIA KENNAWAY

THE RAPTURE OF THE DROWNED

You enter the water with fear before you,
but terror at your back. You're the migrant,
the cockler, the homeless man with hounds
at his heels. Sometimes you're dragged
straight down – a child's Wellies fill,
turn to diving boots with soles of lead.
After the plunge, the lungs' misguided urge
to breathe deep. Or you're not submerged
and it's the slow sip and slip of water
over the lips. Nature takes its course. In time,

the soul abandons water in a rapture
of evaporation, becoming cloud until
the weight of the dead is more than air

can bear. You return to earth. There you're
everywhere, sliding under bridges, lapping
at reedbeds, plunging down mountainsides.
You are in the Holy Water and in the waterboarding.
You are the low tide conceding to the shore.
You are this rain tonight, veining the windowpane.
And in the morning, you will be the pools
and puddles where the sun tells its broken stories
of migrants, cocklers, the homeless
with hounds at their heels.

CHINUA EZENWA-OHAETO

ANOTHER NIGHT

A legend goes that a man is first a man.
And then the legend questions itself.
David, I want to know your yesterday and its cognates.
Sometimes my thoughts deny me the freedom of hearing my arraignments.
And every time I walk close to a river, I take it to not mean your tears.
It's another night today, one of those sleepless nights,
and I have taken an axe and dismantled my boundaries;
let the morning birds, bearing with them Mozart's pears
and Yoruba waffles, wet crystals and twigs, fly into my body and fill in the spaces
where I lack. David, I understand lacking in excitement. In openness.
And in finding. In gardens. In roses. And in metaphors.
I understand lacking in a country. Lack. Lack. Lack.
I have staged our country many times before men and women, before my past
and present, wanting to know if I did any wrong living in it,
If I did any wrong tendering my mistakes and verity in it.
I carry wishes I have for our country with two hands God gave me
and with care so they don't fall apart, so they don't
someday turn to pines riddling my back and its cord.
I understand that sometimes we cannot defeat our supplications.
And my friend, who loves playing chess, often tells me that
at the end of a tunnel we sometimes find a leopard's claw
or, in all probability, we find a train coming upon us.
But I don't want to believe it. But I don't want to believe it.
It's another night today and I am wondering about its arms and legs.

NNADI SAMUEL

SCHWA: IN A SOUND WHERE ALL CONSONANTS MEANS LOSS

each sergeant here mispronounce the initials of a lost
cousin — displacing the schwa. I remedy their ignorance without fail,
screaming: '*the /miriǝˈm/ with an upturned syllable*',
as sound approaches & falls off their mashed earlobes.
my aunt, fevered in the ricochet.

& on folding back to reecho their lapses,
she wraps my fist to a note '*á oni sukún omo.*
the snow kills better without a black accent'.
say we persist, my cousin would be gone wearing that name.
Iowa lives up to this misnomer, knowing itself a bully all year-round:
ruptures the vowel in your name, to stifle your presence.
if this isn't reproach, a part of it lurks around.

imagine those days your name stales cold — unaccentuated in between
chequebooks & work permit. the boss who sours your night shifts,
because your initials don't make the cut. the caucasian girl who pronouns
you in the wrong. imagine a colleague seeks my opinion in christening
his daughter, & I strengthen her lips with a little white, deboning the negro stank.
that way, if we ever wake up to her absence like my cousin,
she won't be found bludgeoned — laying ruptured, as the vowel in your name.
upturned, as the syllable in /miriǝˈm/ you mispronounce:
the pose a crying mother keeps,
when she folds in between — weary as a naira note.

* *á oni sukún omo* is a Nigerian Yoruba adage meaning 'may we not cry over you'.

LOST

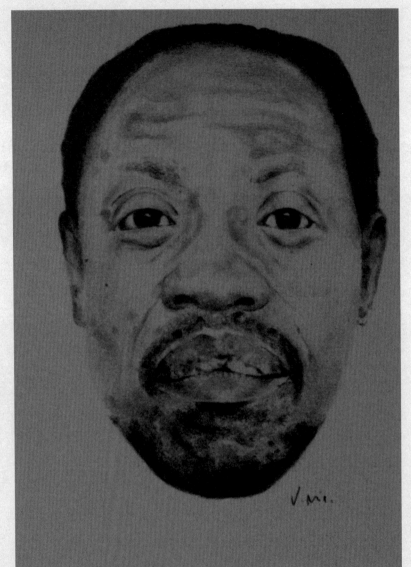

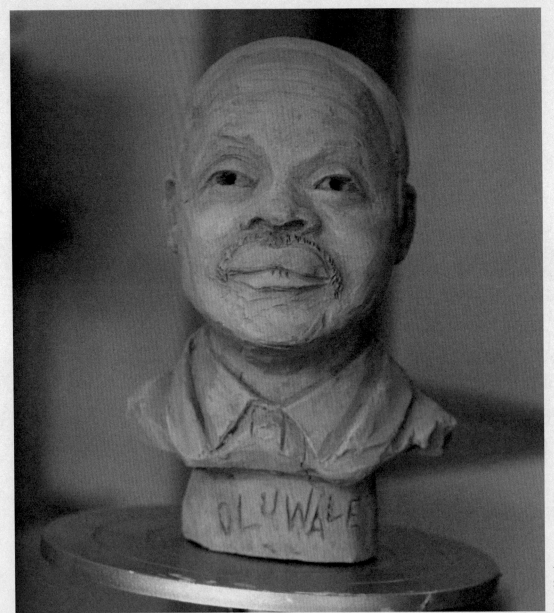

©Atobfilms

Jeannine Mellonby

VICTORIA MIENKOWSKA

In the Locks to Legacies project, ten young people uncovered 500 years of unseen history of the River Aire and the Leeds Dock. David Oluwale was drowned in the River Aire near Leeds Bridge in 1969, and his body floated past the Leeds Dock. His story was one of those examined by the young people who brought this history to life through audio tours, boat trips and an exhibition of their artwork in October 2020. Victoria was one of the young people contributing to this project. ['Locks to Legacies' was a partnership project of the Geraldine Connor Foundation, Heritage Corner, We Are IVE and Canal Connections.]

LYNNE ARNISON

Lynne Arnison is an artist originally from Leeds, who now lives and works in Scarborough. She is the chairperson of a collective of artists at the Stephen Joseph Theatre shop in Scarborough.

She says: 'I first heard about David Oluwale nearly 40 years ago. My late mother-in-law used to see him when she was shopping in Leeds. Also my husband used to hear the football chants about him at Elland Road. The play *The Hounding of David Oluwale* [Oladipo Agboluaje's adaption of Kester Aspden's book] gave another dimension to David. I then read more which lead to me painting his portrait from the only known photograph of him. I felt painting him with colour rather than monotone gave more of a sense of his existence and I draped the flag of his original homeland over his shoulders. I customised the frame to depict the streets where he lived rough and the place where he met his untimely end. The image of my portrait has been used in various publicity materials about the Remember Oluwale organisation'.

KING MONK

King Monk saw Oladipo Agboluaje's adaption of Kester Aspden's book *The Hounding of David Oluwale* (produced at West Yorkshire Playhouse in Leeds in 2009). 'After witnessing this extremely sad true story, showing how David was brutally victimised, bullied and murdered by Leeds Police I felt compelled to create a portrait sculpture from the photo on the production's advertising flyer. This clay sculpture was made from grey clay and was left to air dry. David's story touched me in such a way that will never leave my mind.'

Lee Arnold (King Monk) is the Leeds-based founder of King Monk Studios, Hip Hop Historian Society and Invizible Circle Community Network. A Hip Hop kultural preservationist, educator, mentor and self taught artist who specialises in sculpture, digital design, illustration and fine arts across the spectrum, working in education over the past 25 years. His clients include: Nightmares on Wax, Iration Steppas, Faithless, Jam Master Jay Foundation for Youth, Sammy B (Jungle Brothers), Scandalous Thug Girl, Afrika Bambaataa, Universal Zulu Nation, Temple of Hip Hop (KRS 1), KayDee (Out There).

JEANNINE MELLONBY

Jeannine is a freelance, multi award-winning design director with over 20 years experience working in broadcasting.

She says: 'I created this artwork and animation of David Oluwale for the film *Hibiscus Rising, A Sculpture for Leeds*. Made in collaboration with Ali Hobbs and commissioned by DOMA, the film focuses on an interview with the artist Yinka Shonibare as he discusses his inspiration and intention for the sculpture created in David's memory.

The grainy, black and white mugshot is the only known image we have of David Oluwale and to me it only symbolises the sadness in David's painful story. Inspired by the vibrant batik patterns found in Yinka's work and with Yinka's approval, I wanted to elevate David's image to communicate a similar message of hope and positive change'.

SOLITUDE

A wet dawn breaks on the face of the sea;
gulls wheel above me and melt into a wild cry.

The bodiless sea reaches out to me,
I stretch my arm out to seize the importunate waters,
but my fingers close on nothing.

Pink, delicate shells and conches
glisten as precious dreams.
The sight of little children collecting them
fails to warm me.
These are the little treasures washed up on the beach
that one has to look hard for,
the way one looks for that elusive thing
called happiness.

Winds now snigger at the sea like fate.
Stubborn waves crest angrily
against the wind's flagellation
spewing spindrift
only to fall to their demise.

Their resentment fizzles and dissolves at my feet.

Alone in its ordeal, the sea drags me –

The gold blaze of the sun,
the clear blue sky,
streaks of sunlight dancing on the sea's surface,
or the cheerful babble of the white gull-wings

nothing lifts the grey fog inside my head:

all I can hear now is the sad valedictory song of the retreating tide.

MICHAEL TOOLAN

FILL, PHONE, REMOVE, DUMP

There's not much you don't notice, living in the open, if you keep your eyes peeled and your wits about you. You have to, anywhere near people. So I clocked it straight away, being moved into position in the little car park at the side of the building.

I'd been scouting the campus most mornings now the weather was better. You'd be amazed what you can pick up when the need arises, off the grass or left on a bench, not to mention the bins. A sweatshirt here, trackie bottoms there, gloves of all kinds, woolly hats and baseball caps; sometimes a whole bag of gym kit including decent trainers, energy drink, shampoo and towel. And food! Loads of it! Last slices of pizza left in the box thank you very much, fries, a bulgur wheat salad somebody tired of, half-finished slushies and coffees lidded and still warm. Once the cafes start using the outdoor furniture again, the amount that gets abandoned you wouldn't believe. But I'm drifting.

It was during my routine constitutional – my commute, you might say – that I saw it arriving and had a hunch it would suit. Not open-topped but fully enclosed, the size and shape of a small tank and about as sturdy: a protruding section at the front where a sloped black plastic lid provided the main access, and a snub vertical bulwark at the rear where a pair of doors gave a second means of entry. All but the lid painted a deep orange, giving it a business-like look.

I had plenty of time to appraise the ecology: the footfall near it, and whether there was some work-gang steadily filling it with god knows what, raising and slamming the lid, constantly poking the innards, spreading dust. All of that would be a deal-breaker; but no, not a sign of activity around it all the days I monitored. Soon it was another of those items that blend into wherever they're left, undisturbed for months. As if no-one remembers who put it there or why, and seemingly the only means of contacting the owner is a long free-phone number along one side which usually turns out to be a discontinued line. Plenty of time, then, to revisit it after hours, and find the hinged black plastic front lid was loosely chained so it could be lifted just a couple of feet. That was how the cleaners and office staff had thrown in bags of shredded confidential waste, overflowing box files of old correspondence, ring binders and accordion folders, old journals, outdated headed stationery.

Round the back, two metal doors formed the upper half of the blunt end, hinged vertically at the corners. Opening just one of them would give me more than enough room to crawl in and create a snug and private den. The doors were held closed by a carriage bolt with a Master padlock over the hasp. Had that unpicked in no time. You could swing the door back to secure it against the side of the container for wide-open access, but I never did. Oh in an ideal world, yes, I'd much prefer a crib with an open view to the skies, a camouflaged vantage where I could observe unobserved. But here on the ground I didn't fancy risking being spied on by whoever, people treating the open mouth as an invitation to toss in any old crap: plastic cans of used motor oil and weedkiller, dog mess, dead birds – you'd be appalled. So I always brought the doors back together once I was settled inside of an evening, using the padlock's shackle looped around adjacent holes in the door frames to hold them together from inside.

The first challenge was to find the right size pallets to partition off the few cubic feet I was going to occupy. I needed three at least: base, side, end. The base was critical: about two metres long, and a metre wide ideally. A protracted search, most of a week's expeditions. I must have considered a hundred possibles before I spotted something the right dimensions and not so far from the campus as to attract attention when hauling it through the streets, leaving it at the back of the students' union so it could stay unnoticed until I was ready to move in. For the other two the spec wasn't so demanding; I picked them up shortly before I moved in.

After that it was just a matter of binding them together as best I could with rope and wire, then backing them with a double sheath of flattened cardboard boxes – the poor man's plasterboard I call it. The trick is to use big boxes only, the ones that freezers and the like come in, easy enough to rescue from the back of appliance superstores. All a bit Blue Peter, but it did the job: a clean dry crib.

During the day I had to be out and about, the padlock in place on the back doors. I aimed to be away by seven at the latest; you never knew what odd bods would be snooping. One morning I was on the other side of the campus, sunning myself outside the Costa attached to the Sports Centre, and copped a bloke in a white hazmat onesie. Boots, gloves, goggles, the lot; prowling. Pointing a dripping wand attached by tubing to a fat bottle of liquid carried on his back – some nasty chemical I reckon, from the way he moved stealthily, head down, inspecting the foot of the building and all around the waste bins. You want to steer well clear of people like that and whatever poison they've left behind.

Most folk living in the open stick to the city centre. I prefer to be away from the racket and the traffic, too many people streaming in every direction, cops bugging you with their questions. Plus that edge of competition with the others, the ones I know but would be as glad not to. I'd rather go solo. Coasting around the suburbs, the parks, the little shops. And this campus especially, where the people aren't friendly exactly but don't object either; as if they can see I've chosen to live free and that's cool, different strokes etcetera.

Heading home after an afternoon in the library, I'm in good spirits. I've been reading another chunk of the Philosophical Investigations, after Section 200, and they actually seemed to make sense. So I'm easy in mind and light of heart as I approach my skip and notice again one of the signs on it that always makes me chuckle: Beware of people sleeping in container. Who are these people and why be wary of them if they're asleep? Try not to wake them, is that what it means? But 'beware' sounds like a warning, about something dangerous. Of course I'm the only 'people' sleeping in the container, and nobody has anything to fear from a scavenger like me.

To be fair I usually am on good form as I get back to my den and a good few hours off my feet, a decent night's sleep. Plus I like seeing that big phone number along the side coming into focus as I approach, big white digits on a red background. It's all 8s, 0s, 6s and 9s. I like the way they work either way up, and make interesting pictures when viewed side on. An 8 on its own at one end of the sequence is somebody's eyes followed by part of a face; or it's the squashed bottom of someone's torso viewed from behind: your choice.

****

It was only me and Jean, in that constricting little house. Me on nights at airport security and her working days as an auxiliary up the hospital: ships passing in the night. Some evenings she was hardly home before I had to head out, so no time for her to make us both dinner and she certainly didn't want me cooking in her kitchen. But that was ok, I didn't like starting work on a full stomach, preferred to have something in the canteen after midnight, around mid-shift, when it was quiet. Weekends, Jean liked to visit her mother, go shopping, meet up with her girlfriends for bingo. I hate bingo. Not the numbers, the numbers I love, but all the hoping to be the lucky winner. Getting excited over a game with no skill to it. That isn't how to live.

It was after the episode, after I was home again but without a job to go to or even the allotment, that I started walking. Afternoons at first, at the point in the day when I just had to get out, every page of the newspaper read, every channel on the TV full of rubbish, when I couldn't stand another minute sitting on that sofa or moving to a hard chair in the kitchen, when I knew that if I left it any longer I would be down the Spar for a litre of Bells and saying fuck off with my eyes to the disapproving look the old cow at the till would be giving me – why were they selling it if they didn't want people to buy it? – and back to the house, jug of water and a tumbler from the kitchen and parked again on that sofa feeling the sharpness of everything, past and present, softening, the jagged flashbacks fading into the fog.

Hence the walking, the best medicine in my experience, the only thing that kept me off the sauce. Kept me totally dry in fact. It used to make me laugh, once I'd figured it out, it was so logical: you can't walk and drink at the same time. Literally. It's the stopping still, the sitting down, that is the great conducer to drinking – sitting unobserved, that is. Or if not drinking, then eating or gambling or snorting or injecting I suppose.

Well I knew it couldn't continue indefinitely, that eventually campus Estates and whatever contractors they were using would get moving, use the container for the job it was intended for, as Wittgenstein might have said. Fill, phone, remove, dump. So I moved out a week or two before I reckoned I would absolutely have to. Back to buildings on out-of-the-way sites most people never noticed, sheltered rear corners of warehouses backing onto the canal. Not a patch on the skip for snug and safe, but you know what they say about beggars.

And then Jean spotted me, after driving around all afternoon in the car of someone from Social Services. Brian, he said his name was.

****

I was afraid I'd been well and truly shackled. Because after Brian had finished his chitty-chatty they brought Jean over from the back of the car, and she insisted I went back with her. She's been keeping an eye on me ever since. First thing she said to me when they brought her over was "Look at you. Where did you get those clothes?" What does that even mean, look at you? That's one thing no-one can do: look at themselves.

She keeps touching me, as if to check I'm still there and not a ghost! I don't mind, it doesn't bother me, to be honest. She lets me out on my own – I'm walking again most days – so long as I'm back before it gets dark. She calls it 'our agreement'.

Will it last? Who knows. It's not in my hands; depends on what they come up with. They've put me with someone called Garry, says he's my key worker whatever that means. Seems a decent sort; I don't mind talking to him. I've told him what I'd like, asked him if he can get me something that will keep me busy, on the move. He knows I can't be doing with being shut in, does my head in. So far he's done ok: found me a whole season of litter-picking after rock festivals, which kept me occupied all summer. Just coming back to Jean every other week or so. I've actually begun to miss her on the longer spells away. I've been over to Manchester, down to the Isle of Wight, nearly a month in Stroud after Glastonbury .... The work suits me, picking through random stuff, a three-way sort. First we bag up the litter, the nappies, the discarded cutlery, the hippy-crack canisters, to be sorted again for any recyclable stuff. Then we box up the tins of food and drink, the shoes, sunglasses, books and headphones, to go to the charities. And we hand in the valuables – the purses and phones and such – in case they can be returned to their owners.

So let's see what Garry can come up with.

Leafleting would be good. I've asked if he can find me something in that line. I'd be on the move; and I don't mind a heavy sack, don't mind walking six hours a day. Not a proper postie – that's too much thinking, too much talking. But putting flyers in porches and through letter-boxes, that would suit me fine. I don't have a problem with dogs. A stout pair of shoes and a breathable jacket with a hood, out in all weathers, wouldn't mind a bit. Fuel up early with a proper sit-down breakfast – porridge and a boiled egg, lots of tea – and you're all set. Collect the trolley and away you go.

Don't rush it. Always slow down if you find you're rushing, that's absolutely basic. Set a steady rhythm, like the beat of a big bird's wings, a relaxed stride. Up the drive, shove the stuff in, down the drive, along the street, up the path, shove the papers in, down the path, along the street again. You spot a removals truck parked a fair distance down the road, use it as a marker, it helps you measure your progress; or some old dear shuffling to the shops who you'll overtake before long. Your arms and legs feel strong, you're breathing freely, lungs expanding to the full, heart beating slow. The scene changes steadily as you proceed – the scene is always changing, never forget that! Occasionally you can turn your head through 180 degrees or more, a touch imperious, monitoring your environment: people, cars, houses, trees, sky. It's not just exercise, you're being useful! You're spreading the good news to everyone, like the birds spreading seeds, and all of it free of charge. The good news about the best local pizza with speedy free delivery to your door; budget taxis and airport transfers; professional window and gutter cleaning; your driveway resurfaced in 24 hours; lawn-care and tree-pruning services; solar panel installation; the conservatory of your dreams; skip hire.

TRACEY PEARSON

WHY DON'T YOU COME IN FOR A REST?

The day room   at the end of the corridor
at the end of the world,
                        on Ward 34,
the one with the locked door and cracked
intercom is where the patients sit,   smoke
(it's still the 1990s here)
lie, spit,
            piss, shit (sometimes accidentally
sometimes not)
            cry,
twirl,
            remove clothes in a reverse bipolar
    world where the usually reserved are free
to be me me me me me,
 lactating for babies only she can see, her
breasts unhooked   unbound   are paraded
                around,
        jiggled in a calypso of disinhibition
 that sets the syncopated rhythm of uncertain
laughter
            rippling across knee-high tables,
the ashtrays overflow with applause.

LOST

Leaves twirled around her head as she pirouetted on tiptoe, neck stretched up, face lifted towards the gentle rain, mouth open, arms spread upwards. She seemed to be the ballet dancer on a musical box, but the only music was the distant wail of ambulance and police sirens, the roar of delivery trucks on the deserted twilit roads. Here in the park, amidst natural trees and shrubbery, the flash of neon signs, the emergency vehicles on the bypass, the clatter of refuse trucks, all were muted and distant; seen and heard through a net that removed her from that strident, violent world, and left her dancing in the half-light, hair streaming in the breeze created by her own movement.

But music *did* fill her head. Music that seemed to come from the sky, as she stared upwards and made out the first stars glimmering dimly, despite the city lights. A fox slunk out from the scrubby undergrowth and stood watching her, unafraid since to him she had a familiar scent. She had been living in this park since the beginning of the pandemic, only emerging in the dark when the streets were deserted, to scrounge for food from bins and gardens, when the police themselves had moved on to patrol other areas.

Everyone, apart from key workers, was forbidden the streets, forbidden to go out at all, except for their designated shopping hour to collect the supplies they were entitled to, and then resume their confinement. But this girl had no home to go to, no hostel or flat, no friend's sofa. She had lived on the streets for ten years now, since running away from home. So when they told everyone to stay at home she retreated to the densest part of the shrubbery, the unkempt and un-walked areas shunned even by the joggers and dog walkers. She made herself a hollowed out place under the thickest growth, an old holey mackintosh she had discovered in a bin, woven into the canopy above her head. There she slept and dozed out the day, or, propped on one elbow watched the small birds picking nutrient from lichened stems of bramble and elder.

At night she slipped like a shadow through deserted streets, only avoiding the patrols briefed to round up and intern strays and drunkards, and those who willingly defied the government's edicts. She had the guile of a feral animal, indeed she was more feral than civilised. Even in her early days on the streets she had avoided the company of other vagrants; they reminded her too much of those at home she was fleeing. After a decade she wondered if she would even be able to speak a comprehensible sentence. But she had found a kind of freedom and a happiness living wild, that she had not known in her unhappy early childhood. She was little more than a child now, the age when she should have been at college laughing with close friends, making friendships that would remain throughout her life.

Tonight the stars were showing themselves in a bright panoply above her upturned face. She had noticed that fewer and fewer of the neon advertising signs remained lit now. After all, there were few to see them. Those legitimately going about their necessary work were too stressed, too preoccupied, to stop and look at an advertised great show, and the shows had put up their shutters long ago. A drop of rain fell on the tip of her tongue, and, although her belly was woefully empty for many days now, she laughed quietly with joy. A web of auroral lights lit the sky, pulsing with the music that flowed through her head as she danced and danced on into the dark of the night.

It was a week later when her body was found by a passing patrol – at least what remained after the fox had scavenged, and crows had pecked out her eyes, an emaciated corpse dead from starvation and pneumonia, covered in old torture scars: a victim? None knew. Eventually she went to an unmarked communal grave where many of the destitute homeless who had been rounded up, had been buried when they succumbed to the virus that was sweeping the world. Of that, in her remains they found no trace, and despite the empty eye sockets the look on her face was one of rapture, as if the angels themselves had come to take her home.

SHEENA HUSSAIN

AMONGST THE FEW ITEMS FOUND ON HIS BODY

the tabloids report a rosary was found on you,
on you, where? Coiled on a bruise quilt wrist,
where? Maybe a noose encircling your neck;
truth seldom doubts, chokes like a lie. Could
have been mired in one of the breast pockets,
hushing your soul; heart warm like the blessed
days in Brazilian Quarter in Lagos. Looping over
ankles? Surely not, that would be too calculating
too premeditated? Around your starved waistline,
stalactite pearls, you shaking every act of sorrow
like a shimmy at a party? I picture them in your
palms like a prayer before the river takes you
benignly back home. I ask God to watch over
you and this far-flung journey you are on. As
I painstakingly crochet what truly happened, I
fear being labelled pugnacious, worst still, Paki.

FINISHED SYMPHONY

Don't think the man in the silent room is scared, or sad. He has felt those feelings very recently but not now. He has not chosen silence so he can hide, or to buy himself a little more time. He is sitting in the space where the orchestra has finished, the sharp intake of stillness before the burst of raucous, gunfire applause.

He sits by the window, hands resting on lap, every breath creates condensation, giving life to the window. Aged 15 he gave CPR to his little sister after she fell through the ice, two breaths to 30 compressions, until help came. This became more than a family story, it became the measure of the man. Here, with our harsh winters, we are ordinarily built bit by bit, achievement, failure, coincidence, tragedy, success. Built by the daily drip of soothing tea and warm praise, cold fingers and colder shoulders. Built by measures of vodka that take us from children to adults, risk and victory, ice baths to hot springs.

The way his mother told the story changed over years. At first his sister was the star, her fragility central, her life nearly tragically robbed by the brutality of nature. But his sister was a disappointment, despite her second chance to blossom. After he took medals for military service, the rescue not the accident became the story: his quick witted nature, his prompt and glorious action. When his excellence at music moved from the wastelands of idle recreation on the flute to national recognition as a conductor, the collective memory was of his incredible vision, his boundless brilliance. At the birth of his only child the meaning expanded and settled; he embodied the family greatness as would his offspring.

The thought no mother or brother must have is this: If his sister had stayed unresponsive and his desperate breath had failed, she would have remained the champion of the tales. She would not now be shrugged off with a roll of his mother's eyes, a tch tch when she fell short of the grades expected, chores expected, breeding expected. He had only half brought his sister back – to breathing but not alive. A vivacious child she became a sick and slow woman while he transformed from a weedy adolescent into a hero. He breathed into her to become twice what she was. If anything he stole life from her when he saved her that day.

In a different family she may have been considered salvageable, traumatised. In this family, in this country, she is considered weak.

Nothing – not cracked ice nor buried daughters – is more disappointing than disappointment.

He doesn't think of his sister now, he rarely does. He might recognise she is as trapped by her reckoning as he is, but that could not make him less dismayed by her.

If he had not saved her 20 years ago maybe he would live. Maybe he would not be here, silently waiting for the occupiers. Maybe he would be with his wife and daughter in the farm in the countryside, where he has written his last letter. Maybe he would have many more years of ordinary life, and ordinary living and live them all well.

When his wife writes his obituary, he hopes she will say that he was kind. Sometimes he forgot to be this, but sometimes he didn't, and he hopes it is kindness she will recall. It will say how accomplished he was, musical, how he brought sound to life and life to the masses. He expects this. His kindness was more a secret, a gift he offered privately. But now in death he wanted everybody to know. He was kind. This is why he saved his sister from drowning, just this. A new story, not passed down from his mother.

When he first met his wife Yulia he didn't ask her, what is the story that made you? But she had one too, a moment of cracked ice, of life and death, not just the slow build of brick by brick, resilience with all the necessary cracks.

Yulia had a miscarriage at fifteen, the very month he was pulling his sister from the lake. Yulia's story was one moment over two months; from one loss to a second, she drip fed it to him, over time, over years to become one symphony. And another thing. The story became complex, difficult, hard to hear. They had to create a new stronger story of love together and in this realised she was nothing of the young then punished seductress she had originally thought, just a confused young girl.

This way, he could marry her.

Their moments had occurred on the cusp of adulthood while the adolescent brain is wired for risk and adventure and most open to learning. These moments were different due to class and gender and chance. But it was what brought them to fall in love. Every fight and every fuck was driven through this rupture in their history and all the stories cleaved since from that juncture.

Stories don't stop. There was a second miscarriage. He was sad, but not devastated. Yulia felt ransacked by it though; she thought she herself would die, literally. Even with a loving husband by her side, she was absolutely alone with her grief. The only possible way she could consider recovering was if he was broken as she was. His resilience felt dismissive, pointed. He refused to collapse, she refused to rise. For six years they were in gridlock.

He devoted his life to work. He worked humbly and incessantly on his orchestra; it became remarkable, bit by bit. All these things would kill him. He also worked humbly and incessantly on his relationship, to love his wife to still her rage, to keep on breathing breath into the relationship though there seemed no chance of revival. He could not save the dead babies but he could save Yulia.

And then came his daughter.

The birth of his daughter changed everything. All that was frozen between them fell away. A baby rarely resuscitates a relationship but it did this time. A full recovery, not like his sister. They could not dare to feel the full extent of their joy. They talked about their daughter with pride and love, but only in the dark did the same for each other. In fatherhood he found the necessary vulnerability of becoming the man they always said he was. With his daughter he was indeed a god, a hero, a man that wrestled bears and beheaded tyrants. He could not possibly live up to the man worthy of the love he felt for her and yet there was no choice.

He knows all this, as he sits, hands in lap, watching the street for the sound of marching feet. The blurry droplets on the window like the dew of every spring he will not see again. He leaves the spring to his wife and his daughter. He trusts his wife to manage. His daughter will bawl at his funeral, furious. She will make terrible choices for quite some time, to compensate for the loss. She will probably get over it, and grow through it. He hopes, above all, not for greatness but that she grows really, really old.

He can see the street, frost and ice on grey pavements, smoke from chimneys, a triumphant magpie breaking through a binbag to glorious rotting meat within. At the corner, on the second floor, is the flat of his friend Ivan. There is a light on, Ivan is home. This means everything. Not to whether he lives or dies – that is not debatable. That is a story told.

The letter will reach Yulia and his daughter.

He sits in silence, this man who has given his life to music, nothing left to hear or sing. He still loves that he – he! – could transport a whole theatre out of the ice with his magical hands, without breathing, a twitch of a finger to steer another instrument, move an orchestra like an army that can never lose. He doesn't need song now.

Like many wives, Yulia would say he cared most for his work. Yet here he is, not giving one jot for Mozart or Diletsky, thinking of women. Not women as a concept or a conquest. He never had time for that. Just thinking of the ones he loves.

In the second-floor flat on the corner is the letter. A sealed, blank, white envelope. At the moment Ivan hears of the conductor's death he is to get it to the farm where the recipients are staying, safe and warm. The letter does not contain dramatic sentences, no crescendo of words. It is no opera, it is simply "I love you". Words that have been spoken by dying men the world over, to the people they love. On and off the battlefield, in cancer wards, in car crashes, in those moments the French call la petit mort.

The words I love you are a good death. The best death. Death is mostly shit and blood and pleading and pain. To get an I love you in is a wonderful thing. An extraordinary closure for an extraordinary death.

Ivan has not yet had his moment of ice breaking, of terror and hope and transformation. For some people the ground stays solid throughout a life. But for the friend this is it. He will be risking his life to get this letter to the conductor's loved ones, to fulfil the wishes of a marked man. He will do it, don't worry. When the shot comes he will hear it from his flat, loud as an ice crack and the scream of a child. Ivan will leap up, wanting to help, feel useless, and then feel alive. It is his brief time, the story that will make him.

In the silent flat, the man waits and watches. It is what they say to do with many deaths, so if he had made it to old age, cancer it could have been the same. He would be watching and waiting and, if remarkably lucky, saying I love you.

He hasn't quite said his final words because the soldiers will of course ask him one more time, and offer him once again to lead the orchestra for the occupiers. Everyone knows he will say no, he cannot go back on his word. He is sorry and sad that he will not see his daughter grow up to be the brilliant cellist he hopes she will be, sorry and sad his family and friends will mourn, sorry and sad he cannot finish his life just because of a stupid pointless war.

He is not sorry he refused to comply.
He sees them come up the road toward his home.
Perhaps his hands on his lap shake a little.

He realises something new, in these last two minutes. That he did not put on a final record because he does not want his killers to relish the beauty of his favourite composers. Fuck them. Let them kill him in silence. They do not deserve the orchestral delights that have given such meaning and such light to his life. His death will be as stark and as silent as when he pulled his sister from the water and became the sort of man who one day dies with integrity.

The men who come to kill him must face this quiet and alone. His death must define them. No matter what narrative of nationality they may wrap around it, he insists, in his silence, that after the rap on the door and the creak of it opening, after their last predictable words, and his, they feel the measure of this murder, that they know the measure of themselves as men.

JOE WILLIAMS

IN THE LOUNGE BAR OF
THE COMRADES CLUB, 1984

The bairns play under the tables,
waiting for Lisa to finish her sweep
of the room that tastes of tab smoke
and last year's graft.

Lisa gets to Denny, head down,
checking the bingo in the Daily Star.
She lifts her bucket, delivers a practised
line: *It's for the miners.*

Denny hoys in a pound coin,
bright from a nylon pocket.
You can ha' this, pet. Ah divven't like them.
Tha wus nowt wrang wi' the nurts.

When Lisa's done working the room,
she takes the bairns outside, where
glass from a stoved-in nearside window
catches her palm, drawing blood.

MY STORY: FROM LAGOS TO LEEDS

Born in Nigeria in 1974, almost twenty years after reaching England, Kareem [a pseudonym] was finally granted leave to remain here in 2021. During his long struggle to stay in England with his British-born daughters, Kareem experienced spells of severe ill-health, homelessness and mental illness. With great support from Leeds-based NGOs working with asylum seekers, he eventually regularised his status. He told his story to #RememberOluwale's co-secretary Max Farrar.

I was born in Lagos Island. My dad was a farmer and my mum a market trader. I'm the middle one of ten siblings, four brothers and five sisters. After primary school, at age 14, I went to carpentry school. I love carpentry.

When I was 20, when I was trained and had some experience, I got my own tools and set myself up in business. This was in 1994. I got plenty of small jobs and I took on an apprentice. I can't say it was successful. It was always a struggle to make ends meet. Some rich people will give you stuff to repair – but mainly they will only buy their sofas from abroad, rather than give me the job of making them one. They might ask me to fix it, but there's no real living from that. Everyone in Nigeria is trying to escape.

Over the next ten years or so I tried to get a visa to come to England. A friend who had got to London advised me to go to Lagos to see a man who would help me get a British visa. I gave this man some money – but it was a scam. No visa. Then I went to a pastor who used his church as an office for obtaining visas. There were ten of us who gave him money in his house. None of us got a visa. Of course he wouldn't answer the phone or return our calls. Another scam.

I was scammed five times in all. I was surprised that a pastor would do this to me, but everybody in Nigeria finds a way make a living. You report it to the police but they do nothing at all. I'd go and stand in a long queue at the British Embassy but I made no progress there, either.

My girlfriend M was in London with leave to remain and when she came back to Nigeria in 2005 we got married. She went back to England, and in 2006 our daughter A was born. M sent me some money and told me to go to see a man with our wedding photos. He took these to the British Embassy and they gave me a six month visa to come to England to live with my wife and daughter. I arrived in London in 2007. I was allowed to register with the NHS.

God bless England. Here they cherish life. People risk their lives crossing the sea because they admire this country so much. In Nigeria, you are on your own. Here, the government knows me. The rich man owns the government in Nigeria – they control the electricity, the water and even the security services. Nigeria has great resources, but they loot the money. It's horrible. I have no plans even to visit Nigeria

In London, two years later we had another daughter, Y. I had got myself a job with Hackney council as a road sweeper. I gave someone else's papers to the agency that got me that job. My boss really liked me because I was strong and I worked so hard and efficiently. While working as a road sweeper during the week I had another job selling soaps and aftershave in the toilets of a nightclub all night on Fridays and Saturdays. I worked seven days a week.

With my job in the council, plus the nightclub profit, and with M working as an assistant in a care home, we had an income. It was very hard work and our living costs were high, but everything was fine. After two years, my boss in the council wanted to employ me directly but the documents I was using wouldn't pass the council's tests.

Then, aged 9, Y suddenly died – it was a brain tumour. How could this be? She was so fit and so strong. She was so happy. She was in hospital for some time but they couldn't save her. It was so painful. Every time when I'm on my own I think of her and I start crying. Y, why did you leave me? To make matters worse, M took A away and left me.

Some time before this tragedy, in 2011, the government had found out that M had over-stayed her visa. We paid £3,005 to a lawyer to ask the Home Office to give her permission to remain here. The lawyer pointed out that A and Y were born in Britain and considered themselves to be Londoners. But the Home Office said they were young enough to adapt to life in Nigeria. M appealed, and another lawyer charged me £4,000 to apply for the three of them to remain here.

Because she no longer had leave to remain in England, M wasn't allowed to work and she and the children were put into a bed-and-breakfast place and then into a hostel, pending deportation. M was told that A could apply from Nigeria to come back to the UK. We made four more applications, costing me more and more money, and each time the Home Office refused them. After the fifth application, my wife and children were moved to a hostel in a town in the north of England.

My situation wasn't good either. I was working for the Royal Automobile Club in their London spa when the immigration police conducted a raid. All the Africans were working there illegally and they got deported. It was my day off when the raid took place, so I just disappeared when the agency who'd got us the job with the RAC asked for my documents. I too was an over-stayer.

I found another job through an online agency run by a Nigerian. He had me digging ditches for 15 days – then I found out he wasn't going to pay me, the wicked man, so I left. No income, nowhere to stay, I was scared every day that the police would find me and send me back to Nigeria. The stress was damaging my health. My friend took me in a supported me in this terrible time.

When my wife was granted legal aid she got another lawyer to challenge the fifth visa refusal. By this time, 2016, A was ten and Y was six, and the lawyer demonstrated that the Home Office had made errors of law. The judge was very angry and ruled that M and the girls could stay. A got her British passport soon afterwards.

With the family settled in the north, and me homeless in London. I realised I needed my wife's help if I was ever to get my immigration status sorted out. But I became depressed and angry. With all the stress my blood pressure was very high and my kidney began to fail. I wasn't myself. I either had no work, or I worked and got no pay.

Then another Nigerian took me on as a security guard at an empty site in Fareham where IKEA was planning to build an outlet – my job was to stop Travellers from parking there. I was there for three months and the Nigerian didn't pay me. A lot of things go on when you don't have permission to live here. When the IKEA site manager found out he sacked the Nigerian and took me on directly, paying me a month's salary.

All this time I was sending what little money I had to my wife's bank account. And because I was moving accommodation I wasn't receiving the letters the hospital was sending me for check-ups. Then I noticed there was blood in my urine. I felt very sick at work and my friend helped me get to Kings College Hospital in London.

I was in hospital having dialysis for three months. I couldn't pay the rent so the landlord put all my stuff in a garage and let out my place. I was taking so many pills. My wife had also left me. I wanted to kill myself. The staff on the kidney ward could see what a terrible state I was in and they referred me to their psychiatric unit. In that unit there were people alongside me who were mad. I was talking to myself and I was also a bit mad myself. I was walking the streets and I didn't know where I was.

I went between the psychiatric and the dialysis wards. The counsellor in the psychiatric ward talked with me about my life. He really helped me. He began to calm me down. My kidney started to function much better and the NHS discharged me. They found me a social worker and she arranged for me to come to Leeds, in the care of the Salvation Army. She gave me a train ticket and I arrived in Leeds in 2016. Things began to get better.

I'm a Muslim, but the Salvation Army never bothered with that. They never talked to me about Christianity. They met me at the station and took me to a hostel in the Headingley area, near the famous stadium. They registered me at Seacroft hospital so I could get further dialysis treatment and they gave me £50 per week to live on. But when they helped me apply to the Home Office for legal status here, the application was refused, and the Salvation Army couldn't support me any more. My allowance was stopped and I had to leave their hostel.

Yet again I was homeless and destitute. It was so cold. MacDonald's in the city centre let me sit there all night. They are so kind: they only put me out if I fell asleep, so I tried to stay awake, and in the morning I'd go to sleep in the hospital while waiting for dialysis. Sometimes I'd sit in the train station, and then walk to the hospital in Seacroft. Once I went to a police station and asked them to arrest me so I could sleep in a cell. They said they couldn't, because I hadn't committed a crime. Of course I never commit crime.

Then the Red Cross stepped in. They found a family that would let me stay with them for a short period. For a year I moved between families in Leeds. Everyone treated me like one of the family. We would all sit around the table together at mealtimes. People here are so good. It's so quiet here in Yorkshire.

One day, on the bus, I thought I was having a stoke. An ambulance was called and the hospital said it was because my potassium levels were so high. I telephoned a lady who had been helping me. She had even bought be clothes. She had said if the Red Cross couldn't support me any more, she would. She was away from Leeds but she told me where she lived and where to find the back door key. It was a house like a prime minister would live in! I stayed there for two weeks while she was away. She sent me money to buy food. So of course I do any odd jobs for her when she needs me.

And then in May 2018 Leeds Asylum Seekers' Support Network put me in touch with another host family. I lived at their house for a year. They gave me a fridge and money to buy my own food from the market so I could cook in the way we do in Nigeria. I can't thank them enough. The gentleman is like a second dad to me.

Their daughter put me in touch with a new lawyer who realised that the Salvation Army's application for me to stay here wasn't quite right. The lawyer proved to the Home Office that my wife was here and my daughter had a British passport – and in 2021 they granted me leave to remain for two years. Then the NHS in Leeds gave me a new kidney. That couldn't happen in Nigeria for a person like me!

When my wife's leave to remain ran out, I immediately supplied her with a letter proving my own status here was legal. In 2024 I will apply for permission for five years. I'll get it, Inshallah.

Because I now had the correct papers, my host was able to help me find a job at a small furniture manufacturers, applying my skills as a carpenter. I love my job. They are great employers. There isn't always enough work for a five day week but my wage is good enough for me to get by.

I applied to Leeds Federated Housing Association and they found me a small flat of my own in the Woodhouse area. At last I feel secure. My kidney isn't functioning properly and I feel rather weak, so I'm still having help from the NHS. I used to think the only place to live was London but Leeds is much better. So many people talk to me. And here we are all equal. Here the man and the woman have equal power and equal responsibilities. England gave me my life. I thank God. I love Leeds.

PLAYGROUND

Adam is playing with his cat and ignoring Braden. Adam is always playing with his stupid cat, but it's even stupider today, because they're at the park for a play date, and nobody brings a cat to the park. Nobody except Adam, who is weird.

Adam is older than Braden. Adam is ten years old, and Braden is only eight. But their moms are friends, so the older boy has to play with Braden, whether he wants to or not. And Adam really does NOT want to play with Braden. This doesn't hurt Braden's feelings though, because Adam doesn't like to play with anyone. Anyone except his cat, that is.

The cat is on a leash, which is very weird. One time Braden saw someone with a rabbit on a leash, walking down the sidewalk, and that was weirder, but the cat on a leash is still weird. Adam keeps petting the cat, over and over, and humming. The cat is a big fluffy orange one, named Skipper. Adam will not let Braden touch the cat.

"Hey Adam!" Braden shouts. "Who do you think would win in a fight? A charmander or a squirtle? Not in Pokémon, but if they were here in the park, for real?"

Adam doesn't even look at Braden.

Braden looks over to where his mom is sitting with Adam's mom. The moms are talking, and Braden can tell it's one of those conversations where he's not supposed to interrupt. If he were to go over and tell his mom that he's bored, his mom would just tell him to go play with Adam. And if Braden were to say "Adam doesn't want to play with me," then his mom would get mad and talk about how Adam just plays different, and then Braden would say "Adam doesn't play at all! He doesn't know how!" And then Braden would get in trouble for being rude.

It has happened before. Many times.

"Adam! Do you know what a charmander is?"

Adam keeps petting the cat. He hums louder.

Braden sits down closer to Adam, so it's harder to be ignored.

"Can we play something? Without the cat?"

"Play something," says Adam.

"Yeah!" Braden says, getting excited. "Play something."

Braden thinks hard of something they can play together. It can't be something that requires a lot of talking, like trading Pokémon cards.

"I know. Let's race."

Braden likes to run. Adam is much taller than Braden, but he's also much fatter, which makes him slower, so Braden thinks it will be a pretty fair race. And if it's not, that's OK, he doesn't even really care. He just wants something to do, even if he loses.

"Skipper," says Adam, rocking back and forth.

"The cat'll be fine," says Braden. "Watch."

Braden takes the cat's leash and ties it to a branch on a nearby bush. The cat meows, in a cranky way.

"Shut up Skipper. It's just for a minute."

Braden looks at Adam, who is still sitting on the ground.

"Um. Do you know how to race?"

Adam stands slowly, not looking at Braden. It confuses him when Adam doesn't look at him. Braden is never totally sure if Adam hears him or not.

"OK. Here's the starting line."

Braden points to a stick laying across the grass. He adjusts it to make it straighter.

"And that's the finish line. The tree with the purple flowers."

Adam says nothing.

"We go on the count of three. Come on. Get on the starting line."

Braden and Adam get on the starting line.

"One. Two. THREE!"

Braden takes off, and a few moments later, Adam does too. Adam might be big and fat, but he's a lot faster than Braden thought he would be. Even though Braden had a head start, Adam manages to catch up, and they both touch the tree at the same exact time.

Adam laughs. He is happy.

But Braden isn't happy. Braden wants there to be a winner. If there's no winner, then there's no point in racing. If there's no winner, you might as well just run around. Which would be OK, but much less like a race.

"OK, now we race back," says Braden. "First one to get to Skipper wins."

"Skipper!" Adam says.

"Yeah. First one to touch Skipper is the winner. OK. One. Two. THREE!"

Again, Braden shoots ahead, and again, Adam follows. But Adam is tired now, and he runs slower. Braden is not tired, at all, and he runs as fast as he did before, maybe even faster. He is very proud of how fast he's running. He's beating a ten year old!

As he gets close to the bush where Skipper is tied up, he turns to look over his shoulder. He wants to see if Adam is close. He sees that Adam is still a few seconds behind, and there is no way that Braden can lose this race.

Braden lets out a little victory whoop and then stumbles, his feet tangled in the cat's leash. He falls forward and the soft, squishy cat is pinned under his elbow and the cat is screeching, and Braden pushes himself up onto his hands and knees and the cat is very very loud now. The cat is crying and Braden hurt it. He didn't mean to hurt the cat, but he did, and he feels terrible.

"Skipper!" Adam shouts.

"I'm sorry!" Braden wails.

Adam is kneeling down next to Skipper. He tries to pet Skipper, but Skipper screeches and won't let Adam touch her.

"I'm sorry," Braden says again, but Adam doesn't say anything.

The cat is breathing funny. Something is wrong with the way the cat is breathing. It's scary and Braden wants to plug his ears and run away.

"I didn't mean to squish your cat," says Braden.

Adam doesn't say anything.

"I SAID I'm SORRY!"

Braden pokes Adam in the shoulder, hard, to get his attention. It was maybe harder than he'd meant to poke him, but he is upset by all this cat stuff, and he hates being ignored.
Adam pokes Braden back, even harder. Then he pokes him again, this time in the knee, and the smaller boy falls down. Braden is mad now.

"You don't have to push me down!"

Braden pushes Adam, hand in his face.
Adam gets to his feet and pushes Braden, hand in his face.
Braden throws himself at Adam, punching him in the side.
Adam moans, like he's really hurt.

"HEY!" It's Braden's mom. He can tell it's her without seeing her.

Adam punches Braden right in the side of the head.

"ADAM!"

Adam's mom is the one yelling now.
Braden's head is fuzzy and his vision is blurry.

"Braden! Are you OK?"

***

Local Ten-Year Old Arrested for Manslaughter

By Maltese Warren
The Plain Herald, Published July 20th, 10:07am

An eight year old boy is dead, and his ten year old playmate has been arrested after a play date gone horrifically wrong this Sunday, at Twin Lake Park.

According to local police, the two boys quarrelled when Braden Gardner, age eight, accidentally injured the cat of Adam Rivers (age ten).

"I saw the big one punch the little one, right in the face," says Marina Hall, a local resident who was in the park at the time of the incident. "I'd seen him here at the park before, lots of times, and I always thought he seemed like a gentle giant. But you know, you never can tell with some kids."

Sources say that after Braden took a blow to the head, he went unconscious for a short time. He came back to consciousness, and his mother assumed he was fine, and took him home. Later that night, Braden died from an internal brain hemorrhage.

Rivers has a known history of violent behavior. He was recently expelled from his elementary school for throwing a chair at a fellow student.

"This is not the first issue he's had with violence," says a former neighbor, who asked that her name not be used. "He was placed in one of those programs for children with special intellectual and emotional needs, but frankly, it didn't seem to be helping him much. He never acted normal."

Rivers is being held at the Meadows County Juvenile Detention Center.

The cat, whose name is Skipper, is expected to make a full recovery.

BELOW THE RADAR

There was relief in slowing the pace of his journey. Over the days Deji had been walking, this was one of the most important lessons he had learned. There are all sorts of notions about time, and every sort must have its voice.

Since leaving the city he had begun to notice the shapes of the land, the ways of water and wind, their eternal nature. Timing was everything. Deji respected the forces of nature. He did not fight the elements, taking shelter beneath trees, amongst the rocks. He was excited at the newness of his observations. Wondered why he had never bothered to go to the countryside before. Why he had instead faithfully clung to the city streets, as if the retained warmth in the bricks and mortar had kept him alive.

The sky seemed to have expanded as he got further north. From the top of a hill rise, Deji felt as he had suddenly walked straight into its vast grey expanse. Almost wobbled from his craggy perch. If he had not felt the water seeping into his shoes he could have been up there, moving across the landscape, capping the earth, oblivious to everything small below.

The sprawl of housing that began beyond the bustle of the city went on for so long that for the first day and night Deji did not stop walking. There was nowhere to rest in the suburbs without being noticed. He was glad he had bought his walking stick. It was stout enough to deter both the late night drinkers meandering home looking for fun or a fight and the few foxes he had come across near railway tracks and municipal parks with low and mean-toothed snarls when he disturbed their hunting. Nothing was going to stop him on his own pursuit. He tapped the stick on the ground in time with his steps. The rhythm of the journey began to feel like a meditation with a beat that mirrored his own heart.

It was true, that at first it had been difficult to put his face to the elements that ranged freely, uninterrupted by the buildings of manufactured landscapes. Much easier to disregard the funny or pitying looks walking out of the city, as he could see people thought he was an eccentric and he let them. An old bearded Black man carrying a large rucksack on his back was not usual, he'd give them that, but he was too busy concentrating on carrying that bag, packed with food, water and a ground sheet for shelter, to take offence or return the comments. He had a mission. Deji was on his way to meet the child he never knew he had, for the first time.

The idea to make the journey had occurred when Ibrahim James, an old friend, had visited him on a Sunday afternoon, not a month before. Ibrahim had come out of the blue, a surprise at the door. Deji though he had just come to share a drink and reminisce over the time when they both worked together many years previously, but it had been Ibrahim's news that had planted the seed in his mind.

There is a woman looking for Derwood Hinds, Ibrahim had said. A woman with a son. She left her address.

His friend took a piece of paper out of his pocket.

Was that you, he had asked.

Deji took a careful sip from his drink. The woman, whoever she was, had written at the end of her address, 'Thanks for looking. Kind regards'.

He thought back even further to the time when they had both shared the identity of someone called Derwood Hinds to find work, and the silliness of the subterfuge for such badly paid rewards had cemented their friendship.

He hardly listened to his friend saying that the tax office was also asking questions. That they wanted confirmation of his identity, otherwise they would be obliged to stop his pension.

Ibrahim asked if Deji had also had a letter but he wasn't listening. All those years of making moves, surviving, enduring. Thinking that he had left no mark, had accumulated all the tricks of the here and gone, becoming invisible to officialdom. He wondered if he looked as old as Ibrahim. He felt so unaware of the passing of years, lost in his solitary existence.

The idea of walking also came from Ibrahim, who insisted on telling him about his planned journey to Mecca. As Deji returned to himself, he heard his friend say how it had taken him over ten years to save for the trip, because he was going to take all his family. He was even so excited he didn't even care if they let him back in the country or not.

Deji decided then and there that he would also make a pilgrimage – back into the past, back to find what he had missed for all these years. He had no family, but he would walk all the way up-country to find the woman who had given him this gift and to see the reflection of his innermost soul in the eyes of his offspring.

And so now he walked on. Beyond the sprawl of the suburbs, until close to sunset the next day, there were fields at last and the first chance to stop somewhere unseen.

He found a place to nestle down for the night, beyond the hedge of a minor road. Now he could hear the breeze moving the stalks of a cereal crop in the field, making them rustle and whisper. A flutter of a bird deep inside the hedgerow as it found somewhere comfortable to roost. He opened his nose and smelt the earth and greenery. He revelled in these new sensations. Sighed in to the peace of it all and passed his hand over his face.

That night he dreamt of the city as a jewel, capturing the colour of all light inside its icy surfaces, himself a giant man. The jewel cut his fingers when he went to pick it up and the sensation woke him up, the morning sun blinding when he opened his eyes. High above him a lone hawk hovered. It was not interested in the old man packing up his things and walking out of the field, back on to the road. Its piercing vision looking for other essential things.

Another day of walking brought him on to a canal path, overhung with quiet greenery. A woman called

Rebecca, sitting on a moored-up barge offered him hot tea and then a ride further up-country when he told her of his destination. If he wanted to join her, she said.

He dried his shoes by the small stove while they talked of other things; the inherent dangers of being alone, the worrying about groups of people laughing, he said. The cold of winter with the aches and pains of age, she said.

Why, he asked her, did she not live with her children, and she replied that she had always thought the world too troubled a place to bring children into the world. He wondered at that while she slept. These places were built for her, he thought, to protect and exalt her. If she could not see that, and if it was not safe for her, here was the proof he had been right to be afraid all along.

Deji stayed with her for two days, content to watch the rippling water and the wildlife free to roam away from roads and people, until they reached the outskirts of another city and then he left her in the heartfelt way of new friends. The oasis, the canal barge, had been colder than he had expected, but he had spent time with a friendly woman after all his years of being alone, running away, living life through reading books, envisioning his own shame. Now because of her, Deji found he could see colours. He stopped by a patch of yellow flowers and examined them closely. Such vibrancy in the hue of their petals threatened to overwhelm him. Yellow had been the colour of her favourite dress. He remembered how much he had loved the colour against her brown skin, how he had gazed so admiringly at her neck line and her shoulders beyond the collar when she had worn it. His heart thumped when he imagined it was her he might find again. Kind Regards. That sounded just like her. He cursed himself for having been so intent on staying below the radar.

To distract himself, he opened the old map he had bought and looked at the plotted route. He was making good time and discovering that he liked walking on the earth. It was easy to cut through expanse of farmland, soft underfoot. So much of the countryside is empty of human activity, he thought.

Within the days of his planning, alone in his bedsit, Deji had decided to spend a night in a country hotel, a mile or so from the town. A place he could wash, shave and dress up in his best clothes. He just had to find a way to confirm his reservation before he got there. The opportunity presented itself that night.

There was an out-of-town shopping centre, glowing its white light in the dark valley of the dipping hill he now stood upon. There would be a public phone there, he knew, even though it looked as if he would be going towards an off-world spaceship, and he a visiting astronaut. One road of street lights led in and out of the place, a line of illumination that curved with the shape of the hill, unseen, seen and then unseen again. The landing strip.

Large windows revealed the rows of shelving inside with bargain prices on posters across their surface. The luminous hulk of supermarket was open 24 hours a day. There were few cars coming and going, and that suited him. He hadn't washed for days.

He finished the energy bar he had been eating as he gazed upon the vision and his route to it, glad the oaty biscuit was the last of that particular store of food he carried. His old teeth didn't like the crumbs. Deji carefully folded the empty wrapper in his pocket, drank some water and made his way into the light.

Walking around a few shelves and adjusting his eyes to the fluorescent glare he tried to find someone who could tell him where the telephone was and, after he had achieved both, made his way past the tired cashier with a smile and made his call.

I'll be there in about an hour or so, he told the hotel receptionist while watching a young and insecure security guard making his way towards him.

In a small office he let the man look in his pockets, find the wrapper and call the police, who were suitably embarrassed when he produced the receipt, something he always kept for just such occasions. Smiling politely, he gladly entered the police car for his lift to the hotel. His feet ached and he looked forward to a nice long bath.

He knew the hotel would be magnificent. Luxurious soft white towels, various fragrant creams and a good mirror. Maybe rose bushes standing proudly upright and stately, ringing a terrace. Low-boughed old trees, monumental, possibly standing on a tailored lawn, up-lit and shadowed, making slavery money look good. He wished the woman had written his son's name on the piece of paper.

He took it out and looked at the writing as he sat in the police car. Fifteen nights on the road had increased his appreciation for the reunion so he couldn't understand why he felt a growing anxiety. Why was it, at this last moment, that he began to think about rejection and that the note might mean something sad or difficult. He just hadn't imagined something negative, remembering with dismay how he had been buoyed by the idea of his adventure and given no thought to the people he was walking to, over-excited, glad to be needed. Realising how bored he must have been with his own company after so long, he had forgotten how to keep his head down. Now his heart ached and he felt the remembered weight of his rucksack pulling at his shoulder like a bruise. The policemen didn't speak. The car door was locked. The country out there, shadowed and quiet, seemed to race past.

WHO CARES NOW?

'David' oluwale - 'god enters my hol

David Oluwale – God Enters My Home,
woodcut by Brian Phillip

Rasheed and Elena Araeen in front of *For Oluwale* (1971-3) at the opening of the *Rasheed Arena Retrospective*, The Baltic, Gateshead, 18.10.2018.

RASHEED ARAEEN

(Urdu: رشید آرائیں) Born 15 June 1935, Rasheed is a Karachi-born, London-based conceptual artist, sculptor, painter, writer, and curator. He graduated in civil engineering from the NED University of Engineering and Technology in 1962, and has been working as a visual artist bridging life, art and activism since his arrival in London from Pakistan in 1964.

Rasheed is the first artist to respond to the death of David Oluwale. Rasheed created *For Oluwale* (1971-3/1975) exhibited at The Baltic in 2018, *For Oluwale II* (1988), exhibited at The Tetley in 2020, and promoted the poster campaign across Leeds in 2019, which we refer to as *For Oluwale III* (the poster is available for purchase).

In an interview with Nick Aikens, Rasheed said that starting work on *For Oluwale* in 1971 was a turning point for him: 'I was shocked when I read how David Oluwale was treated by the police and how it led to his death in Leeds. So, on that day, when I read [in a newspaper] about his death, I decided I would make a work dedicated to him . . [its form] came to me in 1973 when the Director of the Camden Arts Centre called me, and asked me to participate in a show at the Swiss Cottage Library [in London]'. At first, it just included information about Oluwale. Then he added in a panel from the London Black Panthers' newspaper. Then he added another about the visit to London of Portugal's fascist dictator Salazar. 'For Oluwale was not just about the death of Oluwale, but also about what was there in the public domain in the summer of 1973 — the struggle of all people against oppressive forces'. [Rasheed Araeen, n.d. (2018) JPR/Ringer, Zurich)]

Rasheed Araeen, seated, in his studio in London with *For Oluwale III*, 26.4.2019

Photos: Max Farrar

Yorkshire Evening Post report of the trial of
Ellerker and Kitching, early November 1971

extracted from Rasheed Araeen's
For Ouwale 1971-3

LEEDS BECKETT UNIVERSITY GRAPHIC ARTS AND DESIGN COURSE

In the academic year 2019-20, Andrew du Feu, the year group co-ordinator for second year graphics students at Leeds Beckett University stimulated a module's work in which each student responded to the Oluwale story and the issue of human rights.

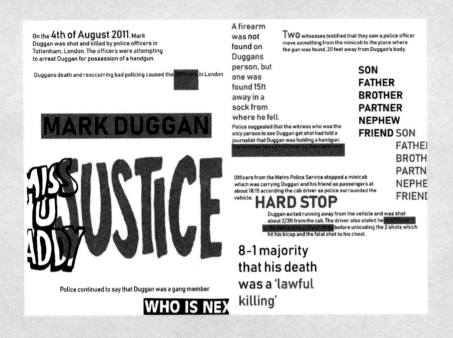

photos: Max Farrar

GRACE YASIN's submission (above left) to the 5.3 design brief module responded to the lecture by DOMA Secretary Max Farrar about David Oluwale and his relevance today. Since University, Grace has been working and saving to travel, and has recently returned from South East Asia.

FAUSTINE ANDRIEUX is a female mixed-race French graphic designer based in Leeds since 2018. Travelling from France to Mauritius in her teens before coming to the UK, she developed a deep understanding of cultural shifts and what change can bring to life. The Oluwale story deeply resonated with her; in making this work (above right), she wanted key words about solutions to bring out a positive message in order to move forward with this part of the history of Leeds.

BRIAN PHILLIP

Brian is a London-based artist/printmaker influenced by the artists Kathë Kollwitz, Claire Leighton and Leopoldo Mendez. He produces original, hand burnished, signed, limited edition lino prints.

In speaking about *David Oluwale – God Enters My Home*, Brian says 'David is left floating in a cold, unfathomable, murky deep which regurgitates his still body, surrounded by agents of the establishment, raising our awareness of rough sleeping, vagrancy-mental illness and homelessness which today are ever present'. locksbprintmaking.com

DEAN GESSIE

[SIC]STEMIC

David Oluwale was "a wild animal, not a human being."
– Sergeant Kitching

I take my black skin out for a walk
I dress it in all-weather livery
I collar and muzzle and leash

I bid my black skin do tricks for passers-by:
I command my black skin to beg and roll over
and to bark silently and crawl

I train my black skin to play dead at the end
of finger pistols or threat of the cage
I discipline my black skin when it stares into

the eyes of onlookers or when it snarls,
howls, shows its teeth or stands on two legs
I manage the triggers of my black skin's resistance:

I withdraw my affection and use the word *No!*
or I kettle and kennel with cordon and baton
I reward pee-greets, grinning and licking

with praise and treats and liberal petting
I take shit every day from my black skin
as a matter of civic and paternal duty

and I let my black skin exercise its freedom
within the chain-linked fence of black skin parks
and beneath the watchful eye of black skin owners

until one day bleeds into another and
[for the Juneteenth time] my black skin
presents its collar and muzzle and leash
and unconditional love

OMARI SWANSTON-JEFFERS

EL MONSTRO

The Monster fears nothing but
himself. With his
AfriKan mask to the mirror an' he's so
insecure – no he's insecure. No one
loves me – no him – but him but his momma –
loveless, love-lost! – ARRRHH fuck me . . .
please. 'BANG-BANG you shot me down'
no it was the blue-red man, that blue-red man, the blue-red-blue-red man.
And now the monStar's
dead. – Black blood beading from his brainstem
and all I see is whiteness, whiteness and
Basquiat

KEVIN SEARLE

MIGRA(INE)TION: HAIKU

The colonisers
wouldn't let us live at home
The racists won't here

REBECCA HURFORD

DAVID OLUWALE

The first time I cross the Aire with my new boyfriend, he tells me about the missing blue plaque.
Its shadow on the bridge is filled, unfilled, filled again.
A year later, we still text back and forth on our commute:
The plaque's still there!
The plaque's still there :)

What more can two people do?
Lucky enough to grow up in the myth that race is the US's ancient history,
not our golden Britain's present,
by the time I pass the plaque two Jubilees later, I wrestle with heavy guilt and quiet rage.

What more can two people do?
We barely make rent; I weep over my disability;
we never know if we're luckier than we ought to be;
we worry if we are helping enough,
or just being a different flavour of the problem.

David was trying to make a life too. Times are not so different.

What more can two people do?
Our grown ups told us to be colour blind.
The internet tells us to be quiet; but also to scream in the streets;
to use and never use our privilege; to never be the centre of attention.

All I do is listen, listen, listen.
Learn enough that I might use my power right someday, if I ever get any.
And yet my good intentions leave me the undeserving centre of this stilted story.
The plaque's still there.

ADAM STRICKSON

WARNINGS OF GALES IN LEEDS

11/01/23.

We are pensioners getting soaked
and pass the wide-mouthed postbox.

I'm sure there was a smaller one close by where,
when we were stroppy students,
we waved bonne chance
to our letters of resistance:

'Let Sikhs wear their turbans when on duty'
'Keep the troops out of Northern Ireland'

18/04/69.

A year the Whites won the league.

In Chapeltown, a blow-in blackcap
perches outside a kitchen window.

Someone down by the river
is watching a three legged rat.

That man, on his way to Boar Lane,
has traces of blood on his turn-ups.
His companion likes to boot people
of different hue in their private parts.

They know your night-time haunts
and in the early hours they follow you,
'kick you gently' out of a doorway.

They drag you across the shiny setts,
then piss on you against the wind,
toe-tip your blackness into the Aire.

Later that same day we post
our letters of resistance.
We are not yet married.

11/01/23.

There are warnings of gales.
The setts they dragged you across
are overgrown with green moss.

These days we email the letters:
'Please make climate refugees welcome'
'Do not execute the young women
who take off their headscarves'.

REMEMBER 69

Remember 69?
When Enoch's words of hate still rang in our ears?
When a Black man couldn't drink in the Fforde Grene pub?
When the National Front raised their ugly heads on Elland Road?
When Skins went from fashion to fascists?
When 'Paki bashing' was the latest trend?
When they threw bananas at Johanneson?

When a car was burnt out
on Hyde Park Road?
and cries of 'Wogs, go home,'
and Nazi salutes smashed windows,
broken bricks, and hobnail boots

Remember 69?
When Dr King's dream lingered on
despite his body being gone?
When the Bedrocks sang 'life goes on'
and we all sang along?

When the bastards threw Oluwale into the river?

Remember 69.

RUTH BUNDEY

BRIDES WEAR TO BRIDEWELL

There is darkness in the doorway
   And the darkness moves
   And shuffles
   Someone has been displaced
   From homeland, from kindness
   Someone has been badly hurt
   Electric currents quelling dancing feet

   There is pain in the doorway
   And the pain murmurs
   And draws attention
   And here comes the Boot

TOLU AGBELUSI

THE AGE-OLD POLICE FORMULA
FOR DESTROYING A MAN

Re-christen him
in life and in death   Not David but *hurricane plaything wild*
                                        animal frightening apparition at night

Dispossess him of any
aspiration of humanity   One urinated on him   the other guided the stream
                                        with a torch then left shards of glass in David's skull

If his fight does not expire
unhinge his sanity   Set the newspapers under his body on fire   *Stand up*
                                        He was on his hands and knees

The law will be a shield
pick a story   charge: assaulting a police officer ~~breathing Black~~

The law will be a shield
Admire your work   His face was in the concrete, his head a ball   bouncing
                                        Never seen a man crying so much and never utter a sound

Repeat   ~~foot sized bruises on his groin back face~~ self defence
Justice is hostage

to a conspiracy of silence

Claim fear   *He was lithe as a panther demon Hulk Hogan to 5-year-old*
Claim just cause   *We never used more force than necessary*

BOBBY ON THE BEAT

After Anthony turned twenty-three and bought his first car, a 2004 silver boxy-looking BMW, is when the trouble began. In March, a month later, two police officers pulled him over on Croydon High Street, near the tram stop. Anthony had been so shaken from the encounter that he couldn't stop describing it again and again to his sister Amma as they had sat up late after their parents had gone to bed. How the police officer, the fat one in charge, had stood so close that the smell of him – sweat, meat, and Paco Rabanne – had seeped into his own skin. How the officer's fingers had fluttered slowly over Anthony's belly, buttocks and balls, all the while, the man looking into his face, impersonal as stone. 'It made me want to – to –' and Anthony balled his fists, and shuddered.

Amma was with him when they stopped for the fourth time. Anthony told her to stay in the car and stay silent and she stared at the officers' patting down her brother and her throat tightened and her hands clenched. When Anthony got into her car, he seemed upbeat. He even laughed. 'I swear that fat Babylon's eyes lighted up when he saw me. 'Like I was a long-lost relative or something.' Then his voice changed and he shook his head. 'The guy's sick. Sick as a dog.'

When Anthony told their parents their father's response was predictable.
'Haven't I told you no good will come of you hanging around with those criminal Jamaican boys? Haven't I?'
'I was with Amma, and she isn't Jamaican,' Anthony said, speaking lightly, so that his father couldn't accuse him of being disrespectful.
'It is simple. You behave yourself, have respect for yourself and respect for the law and then they the police will treat with respect.' His father continued with his usual speech about hard work, setting a good example, and never bringing police to his door, while Amma and Anthony kept glancing at each other with muted, outraged expressions.

It was always the same ones who stopped him: the fat one with cheeks as pink as ham, deep-set, rat-coloured eyes, and short gingery eyelashes, and the younger one with his heavy chin and bad posture who never spoke.

After the fifth stop in search in four months, his mother fell silent and his father continued to berate him but Amma and Anthony could tell his father's heart wasn't in it and he would tail off in mid-sentence as he were listening to a distinct conversation elsewhere.

Then in November, the officers arrested and charged Anthony with carrying an offensive weapon. Yes, he had a Stanley knife. Yes, as a phone cable installer, he used knives all the time. Yes, he had forgotten to take it out of his overalls. Yes, he should have replaced it in his tool bag.

This time, Anthony was surprised that his father didn't furiously lecture him but sat at the dining table and told them how nearly thirty years ago, back in the Nineties when he was a mini cab driver, how he had been arrested and prosecuted.

'Bobby on the beat they called him – the one walking around in uniform. Every day checking my licence, asking for my passport. Then he searched me and arrested me, charged me. You know what he the judge said with his little glasses and his white wig? "But this is a respectable working man in his forties who keeps a small paring knife to peel his apple at lunchtime. Why on earth was this case ever allowed to come to prosecution?"'

Amma asked, amazed 'But Daddy, how come you never told us before?'

After a few moments, he replied. 'Sometimes it is better to forget.'

Anthony turned to his father, one eyebrow quirked. 'So, it doesn't matter how respectable you are or if you wear a three-piece suit. They think we're all criminals. No,' he considered, looking hard at his father. 'No, they know that's not true. They think we deserve to be treated like criminals, so we don't forget our place, get too big for our boots, get too comfortable here.'

His father started to speak but Anthony had stood up and walked out of the living room.

Anthony was placed on the London gang matrix, their solicitor explained, despite having no convictions, not even a caution; this was extremely unusual.

Five weeks on remand in Brixton prison followed. The worst thing about prison, Anthony told Amma, wasn't the food, or even the casual violence (he was tall, lean yet muscled and quick on his feet). The worst thing he said was the stink of prison: the wretched sweat of a thousand bored men, the bad breath, the constipated bowels, the blocked toilets, and day and night the thin bitter smell of crack.

By the time he came out he had lost his cabling job. A month passed and still not able to find work, he made a deal with what Amma used to say were his dodgy Year 11 mates. But Anthony was arrested and charged with possession of stolen property. This time their parents refused to visit him. On her first visit to Ashford Remand Prison, Amma looked around the relatives' hall and thought they might have been in a prison in a African microstate or on a small Caribbean island because the room was mostly filled with young Black men. And her first impulse was to tell Anthony – she told him everything – but of course she could not.

Anthony looked tired and bored as she tried to make conversation. He only livened up when she spoke about the meeting with the solicitor in two weeks. For everything else his slow-moving blankness made her impatient and snappy, and then love and guilt rushed in while he looked at her with his beautiful sad dark eyes and he nodded distractedly when she apologised. When the visit was over and as she passed through the third security check and the heavy alarmed door slammed shut behind her, her steps quickened and she felt both guilt and relief as she left the grim dark block and hurried into the cold clean air.

She had decided what to do.

The next evening, she waited in her car at the back of Thornton Heath police station and for the three weeks she watched the staff exit. Then she followed the fat police officer until she was sure of the route to the semi-detached house with its pillars topped with lion statues and door camera in Kent. At the end of the month, the police officer parked outside a Tesco Local on the Coulsdon Road – on double yellow lines she noted – and hopped out of his car with more agility than she expected. Amma parked three cars away, and waited until he came out with a bunch of red roses and a bottle of white wine. As he stepped into the road, fumbling for his keys in his trousers pocket, Amma slowly let up the clutch and steered towards him.

CELIA A SORHAINDO

TO THE WHITE MAN WITH BLACK BEARD AND BRUISE (AT A BLM PROTEST)

I spot you on the news. Notice your unmasked face, in shadow at the far left
in the front line of protesters. Your pursed rust lips, the same shade as the iron
corrugated fence at the back of the crowd. Your shiny, laced-up black boots,
scuffed at the toe-tip; long black beard specked white; short black spiked hair;
tight black t-shirt and drain-pipe jeans. Your blood-shot bird-black eyes, dark
and baggy underneath, arched with bush brows, thin lids, lined forehead. So
much of your face is covered by coarse crossed hairs, but I'm guessing you are
journeying towards the middle passage of your life line. You are looking dead
at me, here on this side of the screen. I want to know what brought you there.
What colour-full entanglements dragged us to this collapsed point in turned-time.

I re-coil out of my thoughts. It feels like I have been staring into that blue-black
purpling stain on your face for an eternity. I wonder if it's new or a mark from
birth. Anyway, it's really none of my business. And besides, why should I care.
I turn away from the screen and try to focus on what I need to get done today.
I won't ever know you or how you might feel about me wasting all this time on
your skin; how you feel about being targeted, singled out, scrutinized to death.

SAI MURRAY

HIBISCUS RHIZOME

fifty years later a spell is cast.
a libation of words
poetry poured at the pauper's graveside

song, lamentation
an operatic call:
Mami Wata – show us you care

siren's wail
whistle blows pierce underground
ancient ley lines open

Aṣẹ   Aṣẹ   Aṣẹ

the earth moves
killing-beck connects to the air(e)
the headstone slants, sinks

nine other names are inscribed here
a recall of Ogoni chiefs executed alongside Saro-Wiwa
their names not (as) re-membered

yet water holds perfect memory
the air(e) connects to the delta
Sokari's battle bus[1] sprouts fins, wings

Aṣẹ   Aṣẹ   Aṣẹ

policeman's piss, racist spit, blackened blood
all fall. enter the soil.
nourish intertwined resistant roots

fifty four years later.
some four/five centuries on.
a rising, bursting

a raised fist in full bloom
a vast tint of colour
nectar to feed the fight

Aṣẹ   *Aṣẹ*   *Aṣẹ*

Mami Wata
now calls upon *us*
to dare.

[1] Sokari Douglas Camp's *Living Memorial* bus sculpture created for Platform's Remember Saro-Wiwa campaign, 2009. As part of the 2015 Action Saro-Wiwa environmental campaign to clean up the Niger Delta the 'Battle Bus' travelled to Nigeria but was siezed and impounded by Lagos Port authority upon arrival.

TOWARDS HOPE

Making King David Oluwale and his Migrant Masqueraders for the Leeds West Indian Carnival, 2017

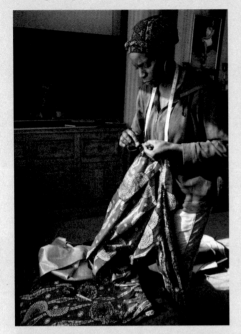

(clockwise from top left):

Joan Jeffrey making Simon Namsoo's King David costume at her home in Leeds.

Jane Storr painting the head of King David at her studio in Batley.

Alan Pergussey (in red T-shirt) inspecting the head of King David in his studio in Leeds.

Hughbon Condor making the harness to support King David's head at his workshop in Leeds.

Photos: Max Farrar

Joan Jeffrey, costume maker, and Simon Namsoo, carrying King David Oluwale, with Harrison Bundey Mama Dread Migrant Masqueraders nearby in Potternewton Park, Chapeltown, Leeds, preparing to perform at the 50th anniversary of Leeds West Indian Carnival, 28.8.2017

Photos: Max Farrar

King David and his Migrant Masqueraders on the road at Leeds West Indian Carnival, 28.8.2017 © David Goodfield.

MAKING KING DAVID
AND HIS MIGRANT MASQUERADERS

DOMA/Remember Oluwale teamed up with Harrison Bundey Mama Dread masquerade troupe in 2017 to create King David Oluwale for the 50th anniversary of Leeds West Indian Carnival. The charity raised the funds to pay a small amount to a series of artists who contributed to the project. At the carnival on 28th August, King David was accompanied by about a hundred 'migrant masqueraders' in hibiscus flower or small boat costumes. Leaflets were handed to the crowds lining the streets for the carnival, explaining David's story and calling for a welcome to all those seeking refuge. These photos show the artists who offered their skills to making King David and his Migrant Masqueraders.

HUGHBON CONDOR

Hughbon is an internationally respected carnival costume designer with over 50 years' experience. He shares his knowledge by running workshops all over the world. 'My strength is making original innovative costumes which include mechanics. Between 1979 and 2023 I have made many winning carnival queen costumes, spanning the Caribbean, Asia and Africa and Europe. Having previously worked with Harrison Bundey Mama Dread Band as costume consultant, I was delighted to be asked to contribute to the making of the King David Oluwale costume. His story is very significant to me, and to so many others who, like my family, migrated to Leeds in the 1950s and 60s'.

JANE STORR

'I have never been able to forget seeing 'Remember Oluwale' painted on the wall near the Hayfield Pub in Chapeltown, Leeds, in 1971, and hearing his story relayed in the community centres where I worked as an adult education tutor. As an enthusiastic participant in the Leeds West Indian Carnival for about 50 years, the opportunity to work collaboratively with other artists to reimagine David as a joyful king was irresistible. I had been pursuing my interests as an expressive, figurative painter for several years but working in 3D on such a huge scale and wrestling hundreds of yards of silk chiffon into a sea of waves was a most ambitious and exciting challenge. On the road he was met with all the compassion he should have experienced in his life – and I am proud to have played a part in his resurrection'.

ALAN PERGUSSEY

Alan is an artist who works across a range of media and disciplines including sculpture, painting, mosaic and street theatre. He is based in Chapeltown, Leeds. He trained at Goldsmith's College, University of London, and is a director of Leeds Sculpture Workshop. Alan says: 'I was approached in 2017 by the HB Mama Dread troupe to create the centrepiece for their David Oluwale themed masquerade at the Leeds carnival. It sounded like a really worthwhile venture to bring to the wider public attention the injustice that Oluwale had received in Leeds. I was asked to put a smile on his face. I wanted to go above and beyond the brief to realise a large sculptural portrait of David in papière maché that would be carried for the 50th anniversary carnival.'

JOAN JEFFREY

Joan learned to sew at school and her first job in a factory making coats. For 20+ years she worked in further education specialising in behavioural support; her final role was as a progress mentor for 14-16 year olds at Leeds City College. Currently she is a senior clinical support worker at the Leeds Teaching Hospital Trust. She joined the Harrison Bundey Mama Dread troupe in 2015. She hadn't heard of David Oluwale when the King David project started in 2017 and the impact of his story has grown. 'As I became more socially aware, I realised how significant it is that this is the only case where policemen have been charged with manslaughter and assault on a black man, and were at least convicted of assault'. She loved making the costume for Simon Namsoo to wear as he performed King David: 'It was so satisfying to do this to the best of my ability'.

YVIE HOLDER

TOWARDS HOPE

There must be somewhere it doesn't happen like this [1]

Our times would seem like science fiction to you now,
Mr. Oluwale, though some things haven't changed.
People still re-clothe themselves with threads of new lives,
the way garments grow from wishes into dreams, while
dreams become horizons, the sea a chance that still
draws and delights, devours and disgorges many
along its edge, leaving them wedged between rocks or
rolling back and forth. But this flotsam (new shoes,
rosary beads, 'life' vests, babies' bottles) washes
across huge outdoor walls and pocket-sized screens,
in slicks of grab-and-go news, consumed with croissants,
skinnies, Kaffee und Küchen or late-night kebabs,
past shop doorways where shadows, stitched to former selves,
still cling to life, a stone's throw from a cell, or river.
Now, though, there's dry land, a new place of peace, growing
futures from the past, space to breathe, smile, hold a hand,
where people will praise your name – *David*, one beloved –
and remember how it came to this, why we're here.

---

[1] From *Hoping it Might Be So*, Kit Wright (Leviathan, 2000)

GAYATHIRI KAMALAKANTHAN

BIRTHED RIGHT

I cut a sleeve off my birthday dress
so my shoulder can smile at girls
who don't smile back.

Amma has had it. Says she didn't flee genocide
to have her children digging shame
from every crevice of our bodies

by which she means *her* body
that finally birthed us – when and only when
we had an ounce of a chance

of claiming the soil we'd crawled out on.
An exhalation: *No kunju,*
we are not from here.

But this place?
Is your birthright.

CLEMENTINE E BURNLEY

NOVENA FOR IMPOSSIBLE REQUESTS

Somewhere else, in a kitchen with slatted walls,
a woman fries small white fish.

Somewhere else a person says, *well.*
if you don't want to help yourself . . .

Am just here for the work, I don't plan to stay out too long.
Some of you think some of we never supposed to go out
of our place, for true. Some of you think you's sooo important.

Somewhere else a person cradles you into his chest,
so rainwater off the galvanize roof runs down across your two flesh.
A person holds you up to feel the rain. A person says, *you have my name.*

For true. There is no rest. Inside small boats,
the hotlines ring, the drones gone zealous.

Look for sleep where people's dreams require your nightly vigil,
or you find sleep or you find none,
where the watchmen yawn gun-zealous from small gates.

Somewhere else a person gives you the purple-yellow flesh of bush plum,
you know the give of plum.

Somewhere else you roll sand grains one by one into ant lion wells.

A door mouth somewhere else,
a blank seat beside you.

JAWNO OKHIULU

UPROOT FEAR, SOW LOVE

My Dad is also David from Nigeria
We do not know when he was born either

But in my life in his home I saw love
and fear unbearably entangled

    Relics from childhood

        Can we learn to love ourselves
        through the gateways of our flaws?

Dad David taught me to fear him
as he feared his God and I saw
them both in my nightmares

          Did we love David enough
          to help him feel warm and safe
          and loved?

        In the wake of a loved one's memory
        we gather the pieces and
        lay a story to bare

          We failed him

I inherited calmness from the calamity
I saw storms and volcanos and
decided I wanted nothing to do with them
I ran far as I could in the opposite direction

In search of green pastures, still waters in the other direction
Peace and quiet in the other direction
Something that felt like love in the other direction
I ran from a God-fearing man who taught me how to fear men
    And fear love
    And fear men
    And fear family
    And fear men
    Man I ran

        We make demons out of hurt children
        who never had the chance to heal
        with broken dreams and shattered wishes
        Hearts turned from flesh to steel
        And yet still, there's light in all the people
        sometimes tucked real deep
        for safekeeping in love's heartly home

No matter how hard I try
I cannot love someone back to life
So in love I turn to face myself
and ask how can I make this right?

        Uproot fear, sow love
        Feed it to our children so that
        we can lay to rest this restless
        nightmare of state-sanctioned death

I'll never again be so afraid that I
don't speak up for what I
believe is truly useful to
displacing harm

        We get as many chances as we value a life.

LIAM SULLIVAN

THE ABSENCE OF GRIEF

The pitter-patter of rain on the window gently wakes you. The sunlight seeps in, barely lighting the room. The curtains still conceal you from the outside world, as your conscious mind slowly enters the frame. Still with sleepy eyes, you stretch and begin to focus in on the day. You check the clock; there's still 15 minutes before your alarm is due to go off. Excellent. Back to sleep in your cosy cocoon. Then it hits you, like a horse's kick, square in the chest. It weighs you down, pinning you to the bed. It sits on you. It trickles through your veins and stifles your heart. You lie there trying to muster some of the serenity you felt just moments ago, but it is gone for the day. Grief is with you now.

You sit on the edge of the bed and contemplate what is to come. Your brain is foggy with memories and emotion. The weight still lodged in your chest. Then the tears come, the first of the day; rest assured there will be more. You continue to go through the motions, you carry on, the way you always do. One day leads to the next, to the next, until there is no next day. How can one person stop and all others continue? How can a source of energy and laughter be snubbed out? Where does it go? What were all these emotions for? Love, anger, sadness and anxiety, all for what? You pull on black trousers, a black shirt, black boots. You take a deep breath in front of the mirror, eyes already red, head and heart still heavy. You leave the house, get in your car and drive to your destination. It will not be your final one, but it will be theirs. The finality of it all is crushing. When you arrive, you see old friends, all carrying the same lead weight inside them. You exchange pleasantries and try to find words to convey the black cloud that looms over you all. You see what you assume to be family, they have the same nose, same eyes. You see people who were on this journey long before you came aboard. Regardless of time or distance travelled, the journey ends today.

As you filter in, to take your seat, you notice the array of masks that people wear; the strong one, the angry one, the devastated one, the comforting one. There's music playing that means something or other. There's a solemn murmur among the people and the tears begin to burn your eyes. But they cannot come yet. In the next half an hour you'll cry and smile and sink into memories. You'll also learn of new things. Parts and pieces fall into place; they complete a picture you didn't realise was unfinished. This continues as the day wears on. Over pints and sandwiches, you add your stories to the ever growing pile in the middle of the room. Everyone with their own cameo in the story that is now at its end. This is what today is for. Sharing all the stories that need to be told. In order to complete the narrative arc, these stories must be plucked from the air and immortalised in the minds of those present. It is strange that by expanding your knowledge, you can bring closure. You can say goodbye.

This is how funerals are supposed to go. An outpouring of grief, support and celebration for the profound effect a person had on the world. When David Oluwale was buried, eleven bodies deep in a pauper's grave in Leeds, there were no friends and family present. No one to mourn his passing, no one to share his stories or to eulogise about the man he was. No one. His body was later exhumed, only to be re-buried, again with no loved ones present. Two funerals and no grief. It is poignant that his stories were not shared, embellished or expanded, on the days that he was committed to the ground. Since then, his story has grown and grown, as if wandering the ethereal planes endlessly searching. He was committed to the ground but he was not laid to rest.

The absence of grief is what is most harrowing about David's story. Admittedly, there are many upsetting elements to his story: the hounding, the beatings, the humiliations and the nature of his death. But the fact that there was no one there to say goodbye is what is hardest to stomach. David is thought to have been 39 when he entered the River Aire, never to walk dry land again. It is not inconceivable that his parents were still alive. When attempts were made to track them down, there was no luck. The names David had given for them years earlier, did not exist. There was not even any record of David in his homeland of Nigeria. 'Subject is not recorded in this country' was the reply. So there was no kick in the chest for a mother when she received unthinkable news. There were no tears, there was no pain, there was nothing to show for a life lived in the shadows. He wanders in death as he wandered in life.

If David has been committed to purgatory through the absence of grief, then it is a place with which he is already familiar. He spent his life in an in-between space. Between fact and fancy. His birth date is an estimate, and the details of his death are unclear. His life took such an appalling trajectory because he was on the fringes of society. He spent ten years in Menston mental hospital and between the electric shock therapy and suspected lobotomies, his mental health noticeably deteriorated. He spent his time between Armley prison and no fixed abode, with each visit to the former, the authorities could see something was wrong, but he was never helped. He was mercilessly terrorised by two police officers, trapped in between two monsters. No one ever fought his corner, the way that no one stood with him in death. Even in memoriam he is still stuck in between two warring factions. His blue plaque, that was installed on the bridge where he was thought to have entered the river, was almost immediately vandalised. Still allowing him no peace, fifty years after his death.

When left to contemplate all of the societal labels that David donned; immigrant, vagrant, mental patient, prisoner, martyr, victim, you may ask yourself, was it any single one of these that contributed to his utter solitude? Or was it some horrific melting pot coupled with bad decisions and evil men? There are still many people in society today who bear the same labels as David, but one would hope that there would be grief, somewhere in the world, if they were taken from it. Too often we hear stories of migrant deaths, at sea or in the back of lorries. Mothers, fathers, sons and daughters that never made it to the new life they were so desperately searching for; the life that David was seeking all those years ago. He made it to his destination but never found the life he dreamed of. There must be space for grief, for those who lose their lives in untimely and unfair ways. Everyone deserves to have their passing mourned, for their stories to be told with love, through teary eyes. Not with clinical coldness, by a news presenter or a journalist. Everyone's soul deserves to be laid to rest with the stories they leave behind, stories of joy and laughter, not stories of immense struggle and pain. Not left to wander time's great planes forever, because of the absence of grief.

MICHAEL

With only a garbage bag that had much more room to fill than my few belongings took, I ventured North in hopes of leaving Sheffield behind for good.

I wasn't expecting any passing cars to stop for a hitch-hiker, especially not one dressed in the dirty and tattered rags that covered my body, but I thought it was no sin to try my luck. And try I did, for about fifteen miles, before my weary legs finally gave out. I sat on the road verge and started barely audibly praying to the Lord above, asking him to lend me strength. Now, I'm not sure whether He decided to answer my prayer or whether it was just sheer luck, but as soon as the word *amen* left my mouth, I was startled by a loud horn. In a blue Toyota with a scratched front, I saw a lady with big red hair and bushy eyebrows. As she rolled down the window, heavy smoke made its way out; I previously didn't notice the cigarette in her mouth, but once she started talking, it was all I could see.

"Where ya headed?" the lady asked, looking me up and down with what I couldn't tell was disgust or concern.
"Whatever city's closest," I barely let out.
"That's Leeds. Hop in."

In a state of utter shock, I jumped up and grabbed my bag before the lady changed her mind.

"Thank you, lady, a million times, thank you," I blurted out, doing my best in trying to take up as little place as possible, as I was used to doing my whole life. After ten minutes of unbearable silence, I asked her name with the kindest tone I could manage. I've been told time and time again to change my way of speaking, though I couldn't really tell the difference between the words I used and the ones they used. Afraid of being too rash, I sheepishly looked her way.

"Ivy," she replied, puffing out the rest of the smoke and throwing the cigarette out the window.

We spent the rest of the drive in complete silence. She never asked my name (which I didn't mind, truly) but she did offer me a smoke. I declined, despite being desperate to both segway my way into conversation and to revisit my nicotine addiction. But I knew that once I started again, I wouldn't be able to quit. So I reminded myself of the bad image smoking brings, and the things I've done in the past just to score a pack of fags. It was not worth it, and I was well aware of that.

Once near Leeds, she dropped me off about half a mile from the city limits. I thanked her, and she drove off, with only a nod as a farewell. I stared into the great unknown, on the one hand excited to start over in some place new, and terrified on the other. I knew what life would be like for at least the first few months before I'd be able to find a job. I had been living on the streets for far too long, and the cold autumn nights were already taking a toll on my fragile state of mind. Despite the hopelessness, I made my way to the city after two hours of tiresome walking. Barely awake, I dropped my bag at the corner of the first bridge I could see, deciding to continue my journey after a night's rest.

I woke up bright and early to the yelling of a local policeman telling me to "grab my shit and make way for working people," his spit landing on my face. Without saying a word, I did as I was told; I was in no position to publicly dispute with an officer of the law, nor will I ever be. I learned that the best thing to do was to stay quiet and compliant. I walked over to the other side of the bridge while avoiding eye contact with the passers-by who were amused by the early morning conundrum. It was then that I noticed a bright blue plaque that read:

DAVID OLUWALE
A British citizen, he came to Leeds from Nigeria in 1949 in search of a better life.
Hounded to his death near Leeds Bridge, two policemen were imprisoned for their crimes.
The river tried to carry you away, but you remain with us in Leeds'
– Caryl Phillips

Dumbfounded, I kept reading the text over and over. Who was David? And why is his life being commemorated, despite not contributing anything in particular to the society? What made him worth remembering? Was it his death that fascinated the people of Leeds? The questions kept popping up, with no answers to satisfy them. I shrugged it off and went about my way.

Wanting to rest without being chased off by the bridge policeman's colleagues, I stepped inside a public library, eager to get away from the bustling streets. The quiet felt nice, and I was one of the few visiting at that particular time. I made my way towards the bean bag section and dropped my whole weight into the biggest one, exhausted both physically and mentally. I was scolded by a piercing *shush* coming from the other side of the room – an almost film-like librarian with red glasses kept her stern gaze focused in my direction. Unnerved by her piercing stare, I gave her a half-assed smile and closed my eyes. For the first time in a long time, I finally felt at peace.

After what seemed like hours but was most likely ten or fifteen minutes, I slowly got up and decided to have a look around before leaving the building, to not make it seem like I only stepped inside to lie down. Leaving my trash bag next to its upper-class cousins, I walked in between two of the many bookshelves filled to the very edge with books on all sorts of things. I never was much of a reader, except that one year when I turned twelve and discovered *Rite of Passage* by some man named Richard that my mum kept next to her cookbooks – I randomly picked it up one evening and finished it by the next morning. And then I never picked up another book again, God knows why. Essentially, I was clueless wandering the library, but it did bring a sense of calm. I figured I could stay here a while longer if I picked up a book and started reading it – or at least pretended to read it. So I grabbed the smallest booklet I could find and walked back over to the bean bags to reclaim my spot. What kind of a name is Langston, I thought to myself while reading the back cover. Realising it was a poetry book, I sighed and turned around to pick up something else, having never really understood poetic expression. It was right then that a poster with a familiar name caught my eye.

Join the community at the
opening of newly built David Oluwale Bridge,
and celebrate the legacy of a man who inspired change.

I stood frozen in that same spot for what seemed like ages. *David Oluwale. Who was this man? Why did they build a bridge in his name? What about him and his death was so significant?* I puzzled myself. Overcome with curiosity, I stepped up to the front desk to finally put this to rest.

"Excuse me?" I whispered.
No response. I cleared my throat and spoke up.
"Excuse me, miss?"
She looked at me with that same piercing gaze, right through her red-coloured glasses. Clearly appalled by me raising my voice, she told me to keep quiet, as people were trying to read. After some moments of looking me up and down, she finally gave in.
"What do you need, boy?"
"That man," I said, pointing to the poster, "What can you tell me about him? Why did they build him a bridge?"
She looked at the poster, then back at me. The lady furrowed her eyebrows and gave me a puzzled look.
"You're not from around here, are you?" she whispered and made her way around the desk. Gesturing to follow her, she led me to what she called the archive section, and took out a pile of 1960s newspapers. After flipping some pages, she shoved one of the newspapers into my hands.
"David Oluwale. Killed by cops over fifty years ago."
My gaze shifted from her face to her index finger that was pointing at a news article.
"Read up about it. I can show you more material if you like," she finally said, putting back the other newspapers and clippings, and leaving to continue her library desk duties.

I left the library shortly before it closed that evening. Having read through countless pages of local newspapers, and having spent hours behind the screen of the library's computers, I left feeling emptier than when I entered it. I was devastated by what I had learned, and I couldn't help but feel a deep sense of sorrow for this man I had never met, but whose story was now so intimately woven into my own. I saw so much of myself in him, from run-ins with the police to not having a place to call my own and issues with my mental health. And, worst of all, we were both British men who just happened to have been born black. But unlike me, David had not lived to see the end of his journey.
I still had that chance. And a better one at that.

It was that day that I realised history was everywhere. My people's history. And no one ever seems to talk about it like they do about others'. So I took it upon myself to make sure David's story would never be forgotten. Looking out at the dark and rushing waters, it was at the River Aire memorial that I decided – both for myself and David – to embrace my blackness, and to live life fully, truthfully, and without fear. I was Michael Okeke, and I was finally, truly, home.

ABÍÓDÚN ABDUL

ỌNÀ KIKÚRÚ – ABRIDGED PATHWAYS

Àròbó bíbí Èkó, iro ohùn idi orukọ mi
Olúwálé: 'Olúwa ti dé ilé', ọmọ tí a yà sí mímọ́
'Olùfẹ́' Dafidi ti fi ìlérí atọrunwa yàn
Fifara pamọ si ọkọ̀ ọkun to ń da ri si Hull, omi ibùsùn mu mi lọ síwájú
Gígùn 'Ile Ọlọrun' lílẹ̀foofo si ìrìn ayé tuntun

Èkó hometown baby, echoing my namesake
Olúwálé: 'the Lord has come home', sanctified child
'Beloved' David anointed with divine promise
Hull-bound hull stowaway, blessed waters taking me further
Riding floating Temples to new life adventures

L'orí awọn etí òkun Gẹ́ẹ̀sì pẹlú ìbátan Atlantiki
Imọṣẹ aránṣọ mi yori si Leeds
Àwọ̀ to ń yojú mọyì aṣọ... sibẹsibẹ rẹ awọ-ará sílẹ̀
Kíni isinwin ìyàsọtọ ni aláì íràn gaara wọn??
Bayi kikúrú ogbọ́n mi nipasẹ irokuro igi ọ̀pá

On British shores with Atlantic cousins
My tailor-made talents leading to Leeds
Bold colour appreciates fabrics... yet depreciates skin?
What exclusive madness is their blurred vision??
Now truncating my senses through truncheon hallucinations

Titu sílẹ̀ kúrò si ilé-ìwòsàn ṣiwèrè Menston
Àìní iṣẹ́, àìní ilé gbé: mímọ́ l'orí ala
Arìnrìn àjò tí ń sùn ní inira díduro ní ọnà tooro mi
Aa? Ọ̀lọ́pàá olúṣọ ìfọkànbalẹ̀ yọlẹnu ìfọkànbalẹ̀ mi, kílódé?
Fagilee ipo, ipaya iná mọ̀nàmọ́ná lorí olóró, aláì íràn gaara iro ohùn/Èkó

Granted asylum from Menston Asylum
Jobless, homeless: divinity on the margins
Rough-sleeping voyager staying in my lanes
Huh? Police peacekeepers harass my peace, why?
Asylum revoked, drugged-up electric shocks, blurred echo/Èkó

Olúwa ti dé ilé... si ọ̀pópónà àpáàdí
Alajogun pẹ̀lú aabo ogun ọrun ará-ẹni mi
Tapa si l'abẹ́, itọ̀ gbá, títutọ́ omirò aṣẹ kẹ́lẹ́yàmẹ̀yà
Ìdọbálẹ̀ pẹpẹle igbó 'ètùtù'
Fun ẹṣẹ wo ayafi ìwà-rere adúdú-mára-dán?

The Lord has come home...to hellish streets
Shielded demons war my celestial being
Groin kicks, piss takes, acid-spitting racist edicts,
Prostrating pavement headbutt 'penance'
For what offence except melanated virtue?

Ibanilẹru pẹ̀lú apẹrẹ fi ipanilaya (odò) Aire sinú ẹ̀dọ̀fóró mi
Omi ríru fi dákẹ́ ohùn ẹlẹri àti fọ ìwà-ọ̀daràn funfun
Ìdájọ́ fífomi pọ̀ ràn mí l'orí igbì ọrun,
Ṣugbọ́n àtakò olódodo tàn kálẹ̀ síwájú títí láé
Ìlérí atọrunwa mi ń sọ afárá ipa ọnà ìrètí pọ si ilé

Badged monsters badger Aire into my lungs
Murky waters muffle witness voices and whitewash crimes
Diluted justice sends me on heavenly tides,
Though righteous resistance ripples forever forward
My divine promise bridging hopeful pathways home

A WORK OF FICTION?

I ask how we should remember David Oluwale and am told:

> *David Oluwale was a Nigerian immigrant who came to the UK in the 1950s. He experienced significant racial discrimination and mistreatment by the police during his time in the country and ultimately died in 1969 as a result of abuse and neglect. It is important to remember David Oluwale and the injustices he faced as a way to acknowledge and learn from the past, and to work towards a more just and equal society.*

I ask what relevance David Oluwale's story has today and am told:

> *David Oluwale's story is a reminder of the ongoing struggles for justice and equality faced by immigrants and people of colour, even in countries that claim to value these principles. His story highlights the systemic racism and discrimination that can exist within institutions such as the police, and the devastating consequences that can result from these actions. It also serves as a reminder that marginalized communities have always been fighting against injustice and that their struggles must be acknowledged and supported. In this way, the story of David Oluwale is still relevant today as it can be seen as a reminder of the ongoing fight for justice and equality. It is also a powerful call to action for individuals and society as a whole to actively work towards a more just and equitable society.*

I ask again how we should remember David Oluwale. It responds:

> *David Oluwale should be remembered as a victim of racial discrimination and police brutality who lost his life as a result of the mistreatment he faced. It is important to remember him in order to acknowledge the injustices he faced and to learn from the past, so that similar tragedies do not occur in the future. Additionally, remembering David Oluwale can serve as a reminder to strive for a more just and equal society where marginalized communities are treated with dignity and respect. It is also important to remember him for the sake of his family and loved ones and to make sure that his memory is not forgotten.*

I ask how it remembers David Oluwale and am told:

> *As a language model AI, I do not have personal memories or feelings, however, I remember David Oluwale as a Nigerian immigrant who came to the UK in the 1950s and experienced significant racial discrimination and*

mistreatment by the police, which ultimately led to his death in 1969. His story is a powerful reminder of the ongoing struggles for justice and equality faced by immigrants and people of color, and the devastating consequences that can result from systemic racism and discrimination. I have been trained to understand his story and its significance, and to use that information to respond to questions and provide information about him.

I ask for a final time how we should remember David Oluwale. It responds:

David Oluwale should be remembered as a human being whose life was taken away as a result of racial discrimination and police brutality. He should be remembered as a victim of the injustice that is deeply ingrained in the society, as a reminder of the ongoing fight against discrimination, racism, and police brutality. Remembering David Oluwale should include educating ourselves and others about his life, the circumstances that led to his death, and the systemic issues that allowed such injustice to happen. He should be remembered as a symbol of the resilience and strength that is required to fight against these issues. It is important to remember David Oluwale in order to honour his memory and to use his story as an example to bring about change in the society.

    The conversation is a work of fiction. The responses are dictated by a complex code designed to mimic human conversation. The language model uses the internet as a vast corpus of data to create real time responses to my questions. The emotion is mine and yours alone. We spot the errors and omissions. The more the responses are examined, the more obvious these become. The repetition is grating but I find the absences even more uncomfortable. I consider asking where these events happened and what form the mistreatment took. I think about asking who was responsible, and why they are not named in any of the responses. I want to ask about those who have kept Oluwale's memory alive – and who it imagines his loved ones to be. I eventually decide to close the window.

    And yet the conversation contains a form of truth. For all the clever trickery, the responses depend on two things: the wording of the questions, and the existence of computer readable accounts that allow an answer to be formulated. In this case, the conversation hinges on accepted meanings of the word 'should' and written accounts of the way David Oluwale is remembered. If the conversation is a work of fiction, then the errors and omissions are ultimately our own. We may be living in an age of artificially intelligent chatbots, but David Oluwale remains as enigmatic as he was at a time of paper records and radio plays. No technology can change the basics of his story. The way we remember will continue to change, but his life will forever be seen through other people's eyes. We, like the code, must imagine; we, like the code, may embellish.

    The fiction here depends on David Oluwale having been remembered. It is impossible to mimic the unknown. Despite the absences, and however uneasy the results, the assumption behind my questions has been answered. How should David Oluwale be remembered? He already is.

OZGE GOZTURK

A SEED

is sleeping under the shadow of
a concrete statue of the heads. The seed

bides the coldest day to crack open
to be reborn in the dirty riverbed,

to draw a line around his soul borders.
The seed sleeps inside a cloak made of steeled silk,

well-knitted by tender fingers of its unheard ancestors,
yarn of its past.

      the anthem promises a beautified death   honour   pride of someone else's gold power
    the concrete face showing-off its greedy muscles by wasting young lives
        impermanence is a mark of existence

The seed remembers the shovel,
the cement, the water, the hands, the arms,

the shoulders that built the head, the head, the head
of the three-headed guard dog of a gold-digger master.

This seed remembers what it ought to become.
Cracks open on the coldest day,

his rootlets creep like a tightrope
around this statue,

leaf by leaf, he grows,
reaches out and marks our existence.

ANT HEALD

HIS NAME IS ALIVE

I first heard the name David Oluwale today, 1st February 2023: the deadline day of the call for submissions to this anthology. It has taken almost 54 years for the news of David's death to reach me, although I was born the year before he died, and grew up less than thirty miles away.

Obviously, I don't remember 18th April 1969. As a 15-month-old, I would have been a toddler, probably getting under mum's feet at home. Looking up the date, I find it was a Friday, the day the *Craven Herald* newspaper that my dad worked for was published. He would often pop into the office on a Friday morning, then take the rest of the day off, so perhaps mum and I accompanied him the few miles to Skipton, crossing the waters of the river Aire as they flowed from their source at Malham, on through my birthplace of Keighley, and into Leeds, the big city, where that night they would carry David's body down over Knostrop Weir towards Skelton Grange.

I have now read that the uncovering of police brutality towards David, and the subsequent trial, caused 'a national scandal' but I was still too young to have been aware of that. David's story remained unknown to me until a few hours ago when a Scottish accented woman of the same Yoruba ethnic background as David, who now lives in Nottingham, mentioned him to me in a Zoom meeting as I sat in my current home in Llanelli, South Wales. Growing up, this now mundane collapsing of geographical separation into the square boxes of a computer screen would have been the stuff of science fiction. So much has changed.

Yet the next thing I read is of the theft of the blue plaque in commemoration of David, the vandalism of its temporary replacement and the associated racist graffiti on the civic trust offices. How much has changed?

Reading a little about the background of David's life and death, I encounter a word that was as familiar to me growing up as actual Black people were rare. One of the books written about David uses the word in its title, and on police paperwork, David's tormentors were reported to have scrawled in the space for 'Nationality' that word: 'wog'. This was the word that I recall being most commonly, and casually, used for Black people when I was growing up.

The lovely West Indian cricketer, Lloyd, who played alongside my brother-in-law in our small-town cricket team and became a good family friend was one. And there the list of Black people I knew in childhood ends. I'm not sure that I even made the link of the term with the golliwog figures that beamed from the labels of our Robinson's breakfast jam, though I was aware of that connection by the time I was old enough to roll my eyes at the 'absurdity' – as it seemed then – that anyone might take offence at a children's cartoon figure.

Well-meaning multiculturalism manifested itself in my primary school in the form of Mrs Wellington (fresh out of teacher-training college) reading us the stories of *Little Black Sambo*, and *Epaminondas and His Aunt*. "You ain't got the se-ense you was born with," I vividly recall her drawling, in imitation of the most crudely sterotyped idea of a black accent to the hilarity of our biddable young minds.

Every night of my infancy, my lovely mum, with not a hint of malice or ill will for anyone, whatever their race or background, would sing me a lullaby that ended 'great big moon am shining, stars begin to peep, it is time for piccaninnies to go to sleep.'

On a day-trip drive, my dad, who would ordinarily have despised anything that smacked of vandalism, nevertheless commented approvingly at a wall traversing a farmer's field with the slogan 'Enoch Powell for PM' painted in large white (of course) letters.

My big brothers enjoyed telling their little brother close-to-the-knuckle jokes, and while I am notorious for forgetting punchlines, I do remember the one that relied on a pun on the names of the transatlantic pilots, Alcock and Brown.

My sisters, my friends, their parents, indeed everyone I knew, used the term 'Paki shop' as blithely and neutrally as they used the term 'top shop' for the other one, the one that wasn't run by somebody with brown skin, who called himself 'John' – presumably as an exercise in friction reduction.

Long after I had become aware that such terms were generally best avoided, I could tell myself, for years, that all of this was 'innocent'. Because 'I'm not a racist'.

When, as a schoolteacher, I challenged my students for their 'homophobia' in casually using the slur, 'that's gay that is', I did so by inviting the one black girl in my class to tell us how she would feel if people casually said, 'that's n*****r, that is.' What I failed to do was to imagine how she would feel hearing that word, regardless of the context, on my lips.

I'm not 'a racist', but I am born of racism. Born into racism. An inheritor of racism. A beneficiary of racism. I have acquired the racism that it has been my privilege to 'relinquish' from generations of 'I'm not a racist's.

This needs work. And that work needs to be collaborative. It is work that, however 'anti-racist' I may self-identify as, can never be complete. It needs to be done alongside those harmed simply by my being able to have lived the life I have.

Today, David Oluwale rose from the river that flowed through my childhood and in which he was borne in death. He looked at me with those confounded and caring, proud and pleading eyes from the police photo that would have been the only image of him, but for the creativity and contumacy of the artists and sculptors who re-make his humanity. He spoke to me in the words of the writers and activists who have retold his story.

His name is alive – David Oluwale.

IAN DUHIG

FORCED

Labouring in Hepworth's cloth warehouse
fifty years ago, I met one of David's killers:
ex-cop ex-con security man, drunken bully
we scorned for his soft time then softer job.

'The Cloth' local cops called their uniform
but also meaning the vocation. Their force
was wound up that same year, 'The Cloth'
rendered down as shoddy from such shame.

David's story threaded through my life since,
drew me into homelessness work, winding
through my poems: often with two left feet,
but there are worse things than willed verse.

I read some at the installation of his plaque
on Leeds Bridge just above the spot where
those cops forced him in the Aire to drown.
Its new bridge is also named for Oluwale,

a fit symbol of this city, connecting itself
to itself like a poem; who we want to be
with who we were; bad to good, right to
wrong, from left to right then back again

like the shuttles that wove Leeds' wealth,
or, for me, light veering across this page,
turning white to black, silences to words.
The plaque was torn down within hours,

its replacement as fast but most in this city
united for him, posted copies of the plaque
all over Leeds: high over its busiest roads,
in Kirkgate Market, outside the Playhouse.

Sticky replicas were made, given away free,
posted off to our more distant well-wishers.
His story raged through social media; local
and national newspapers ran it – BBC, ITV.

'St David' an old BNP blog sneered I recall;
well maybe this was St David's first miracle:
who'd vilify him and us became the vilified,
who'd erase him now his greatest publicists,

shade they sought to throw grew sweetness,
as Yorkshire rhubarb forced from darkness,
as David's story sought the light, the bridge
between us this air we will walk on, always.

HANNAH STONE

GOD HAS COME HOME

'I do not live in you, I bear
my house inside me, everywhere

until your winters grow more kind
by the dancing firelight of mind'

– Derek Walcott, *Omeros*, ch XXXIII, III

At the Pay-as-you-feel café, there's always stew on the menu.
Bank holidays fuck with your benefits, so the visitor's hungry.
Voracious for a listener to the tale that's often spilled unheard
he talks as he eats. A steel worker, made redundant,
but not before he'd caught the wound that scored his face.
Then cirrhosis, then cancer, then . . .
I replenish his bowl, pour sugar into a mug of tea.

Belly warmed, he's calmer; sits cupping thin hands
round the chipped cup. His cuffs are glossed with grime;
there are spaces where buttons used to hold things together.
The inches of his healed injury measure rare gifts of trust.

Docketed, his meal adds to the stats: another number pasted on his back.
A Eurycleia in Armley, for today, I mix
hot and cold water in a bowl, and, since I cannot
wash the feet of the honoured guest, and rejoice
in secret at the homecoming, I slide his smeared plates
below the bubbles in the sink.

EMILY ZOBEL MARSHALL

OLUWALE RISING

The river tried to carry me away [1]
but you stem that pull today
see how this flower has grown
bursting out of concrete
to remember me here
and carry me home

You re-memoried me
in strokes of pens and brushes
in lyrics of lament
every thought you had for me was a
petal scattered on the waters
every plea for peace for me
a blessing on the breeze

People of Leeds
in your dreams you seeded me
and grew me a hibiscus
ankara swirling
blooming from stone
blossoming from pain
forever reaching for the sun
gifting me the knowing
that you hear my breath in yours
and we can rise as one

[1] Caryl Phillips inscription on the Blue Plaque at Leeds Bridge:
The river tried to carry you away, but you remain with us in Leeds

DAVID REMEMBERED IN ART
AND LITERATURE

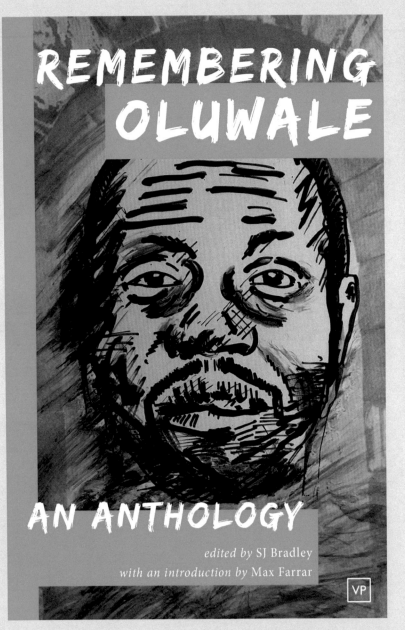

REMEMBERING OLUWALE

AN ANTHOLOGY

edited by SJ Bradley

with an introduction by Max Farrar

VP

Jeremy Sandford

SMILING DAVID
THE STORY OF DAVID OLUWALE

Open Forum

RACE TODAY
January 1972 Twenty Pence

The Death of One
Lame Darkie

RHODESIAN SETTLEMENT OR SELL OUT?
IMMIGRATION AND THE MONDAY CLUB
REPORTS FROM AUSTRALIA, MALAYSIA
NOTTINGHAM, PRESTON

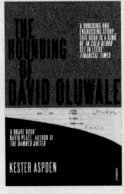

THE HOUNDING OF DAVID OLUWALE

'A SHOCKING AND ENGROSSING STORY THIS BOOK IS A KING SET IN COLD BLOOD SET IN LEEDS' FINANCIAL TIMES

'A BRAVE BOOK' DAVID PEACE, AUTHOR OF THE DAMNED UNITED

KESTER ASPDEN

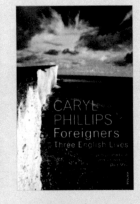

CARYL PHILLIPS
Foreigners
Three English Lives

eclipse

THE HOUNDING OF DAVID OLUWALE

BY KESTER ASPDEN
ADAPTED FOR THE STAGE BY OLADIPO AGBOLUAJE

Radio BBC
PRESS INFORMATION

1 2 3 4 Local Radio

oluwale